Shadows of the Past

By the same author

Breaking the Clouds
A Poisoned Legacy

Shadows of the Past

Margaret Blake

ROBERT HALE · LONDON

First published in Great Britain 2009

ISBN 978-0-7090-8774-8

Robert Hale Limited
Clerkenwell House
Clerkenwell Green
London EC1R 0HT

www.halebooks.com

2 4 6 8 10 9 7 5 3 1

For John with love

Typeset in 11½/15pt Palatino
by Derek Doyle & Associates, Shaw Heath
Printed in the UK by the MPG Books Group

CHAPTER ONE

'SHE'S here!'

Luca signed the letter he had been reading, pushed it to one side and then took up the next letter.

'Papa,' Renata whined. 'Do come and look.'

His daughter looking from the window, urged him with an impatient wave of her hand. The truth was he did not want to look but, sighing defeat, he slid the top on to the gold fountain pen and, leaving the desk, hauled himself across the room.

He looked out of the window over Renata's head. The silver limousine was parked on the forecourt and Guido, in his smart grey uniform, had gone to open the door. Guido put his arm inside the car, urging his passenger to leave. Then he stood smartly to one side, his back as straight as any guardsman's.

Slender legs swung down, there was another hesitation before the rest of her was visible; she was moving very slowly as if in great physical pain and when she straightened up, she put a hand up to her eyes as if the brilliant sunshine were burning holes in them.

'I don't know why she has to come back,' Renata snapped. 'I shan't see her; I told you that, Papa, and I mean it!'

'Well, that's your choice, Renata,' her father replied coldly.

'But there is nowhere else for her to go, at least for the time being.' He looked at his daughter and wondered why she could be so unkind. Why the young girl could not feel any compassion for the woman who had just arrived. After all, whatever Alva had done in the past, now she needed someone to care for her. She had been run over by a hit and run driver and had been left for dead in the middle of the road. Had it not been for a cyclist another car could easily have gone over her again. It was a terrible thing to have happened. Still, Luca admitted to himself that it was wrong to have her come back; at the heart of him he knew that.

'I don't believe it; she just wants to get back with you. You should have just put her in a mental hospital.'

'I would hardly do that, Renata, and it is cruel of you to suggest such a thing. I know how you feel but you have to stop worrying about it. It is not your concern – you will be back at university in a day or so and it would not harm you at least to greet her. Alva has been through a lot. I know it's not ideal that she's back here, but there's nowhere else for her to go.'

His daughter turned huge black eyes on to him; she looked troubled and it disturbed him to see it.

'My being away will make it all the more easy for her to ensnare you, Papa; you have to be on your guard against her. You know what she's like. She's a sly and manipulative liar!' Renata spat. She tossed her black hair angrily.

After all this time her dislike of Alva was still there, it roared away inside her and it would never leave her. The jealousy, the pain – he knew she had even prayed about it but it had not left her. She hated Alva and she probably always would. This hatred was not without some justification, but it was too much now. He knew that as a younger girl she had had these deep feelings, but now she should have a more mature approach. He did not expect that she would ever like

Alva, but carrying the hatred like this was disturbing. It was not natural. There was an intensity about Renata that was unpleasant to contemplate.

'I had better go and see her,' Luca said but there was weariness in his voice and no sense of excitement. Renata seemed pleased by the sound of his voice and she gave him a hug.

'Do be on your guard, Papa!'

'Of course.' He kissed the top of her head and then he turned and went to the door, before he opened it he paused a moment looking with concern back at his daughter. Renata had become thinner than ever and that worried him. She said it was nervous energy and when he was around she did eat. Her black hair was shiny but cut so that it resembled frayed string.

'Renata, do not get so worked up about Alva. I have no feelings for her any more.'

'Good.' Renata turned to look at him. 'But be very careful, Papa when she's around you, you *know* what she's like.'

Luca nodded his agreement before he stepped out on to the landing, closing the door softly behind him.

Alva was in the hallway. Guido had brought in a small suitcase. Of course she would have very little to bring.

Count Luca San Giovanni Mazareeze looked down on her from the top of the stairs. She looked even smaller from this viewpoint and more slender and delicate than he could ever remember her being. Of course she would look delicate, she had been seriously ill after being injured in a near fatal accident. Her silvery blonde hair was pulled back from her face and caught in a French pleat. There were tiny bruises beneath her eyes, more yellow than purple now, and several small healing cuts at her forehead and chin. The consultant that he had spoken to on the telephone had said the scarring was superficial and would not be permanent.

She was wearing a dark navy suit; it was not a good fit, the jacket being a little large at the shoulders, and the skirt at her hips. Her shoes were unflattering pumps but in spite of it, she was still that ethereal beautiful Alva that he remembered.

He went down the stairs; the luxurious carpet softening his tread. She seemed miles away and obviously did not hear him. She actually started like a frightened deer when he said her name. '*Alva*.'

The man was tall and very dark; his skin a warm olive, his hair black and thick and luxurious and the eyes that swept her were the colour of old gold. His features were imperious; the Roman nose, fine sculptured cheekbones and thin but well shaped lips, all giving him the appearance of the true aristocrat.

She knew his name, had memorized it. Count Luca San Giovanni Mazareeze, that he was the *il Perdone* – that this island of Santa Caterina was his. All these things had been told to her in the hospital. All these things she could believe but what she could not accept or even take in was that this man – this man who seemed so cold and aloof – was actually *her husband!*

'You had a good journey?' he asked.

'Thank you, yes,' she murmured softly. It was loud enough for him to hear the familiar husky tone of voice that was one of her attractions. In fact it was the first thing that had drawn him to her, those conversations on the telephone when he had no idea what she even looked like, but that voice, warm and husky and even more so when she laughed, had driven him to seek her out.

'I am sorry about this, Conte, but I don't remember anything.'

'So I understand,' he murmured coolly. His eyes swept her from tip to toe and she felt her cheeks colouring. His appraisal obviously found her wanting for he turned to the chauffeur who was still waiting by the door.

The conte addressed him in rapid Italian, asking for Claudia to be sent for so that she could show the contessa to her room. Alva caught some of it, looking confused at the term contessa but of course, if she were still his wife, then it made sense that she was still the contessa. They were not divorced, that much she had gleaned, but they had been separated for two years. Odd that there had not been a divorce in all that time, yet she knew she dare not pursue the reasons just yet, if in fact ever, for she could not see herself ever having a conversation with this cold and aloof man.

'When you have rested, I will arrange for my assistant to show you around the palazzo. You will not remember it and as you see, it is large and I should hate it if you were to lose yourself.'

How anyone could put so much sarcasm into such a sentence was beyond Alva but it was there. Did he not believe her? Something was the matter with him; it was in his attitude. Not merely his coldness but something else. If he had disliked her so much why then were they not divorced?

She raised her head and stared him in the face. He was quite good-looking. How could she not remember anything about him? He was so obviously unforgettably attractive.

'Could you not spare the time to show me around?' she asked daringly. 'I am sure that would help me more than a stranger doing it.'

'Antonio is hardly a stranger to you, Alva. In fact, you used to be very good friends as I recall.'

Again there was something there. He said the words but those ordinary little statements were emphasized in such a way that they were conveying more than they warranted. Yet how could she be expected to break the code when she could not remember anything, or anyone?

'I have no recollection of Antonio,' she said.

'Nor of me, so what is the difference?'

'The difference, Conte, is that you are my husband and he is not.'

There! Bull's eye, she had scored, his mouth turned down a little and his black brows crested.

However he was saved from replying by a forty-something woman coming into view. She was round and small and dark but with bright friendly eyes, giving a little bobbing gesture to the conte and then, turning to Alva, she did the same but with a smile that said welcome, more than any words could.

'Claudia, will show you to your room. If you will excuse me, Alva,' he turned to leave. Even in the soft pale-blue jeans and dark-green cashmere polo shirt, he was every inch the haughty aristocrat but she would not be put off and she said, 'And you will come and show me the Palazzo, Conte Luca – at what time might I expect you?'

He turned to face her, his expression stony. He opened his mouth and then seemed to change his mind, for he looked at his gold wristwatch and said. 'In one hour, Alva.'

In the wake of his departure, she let out an audible sigh.

'The contessa has not changed.' Claudia murmured. 'I see it, but you look so frail. Come, you have your old room – you might remember – it looks down to the sea and you so loved to watch the sea.'

'Did I? I wish I could remember.' Alva put a hand up to her head, her eyes sweeping the impressive hallway. The tiles beneath her feet were colourful and obviously precious. The magnificent hallway was panelled in fine wood; several paintings graced the walls – judging by their colour and style they had to have been painted at the time of the Renaissance and probably were worth more money than she could imagine. She took note of the frescoed ceiling and the gold-painted elaborate mouldings. Surprising her, a band seemed to tighten around her heart. She recognized it stemmed from emotional, rather than physical pain. She looked up the stairs, the band tightened. She did not want to move. It was Claudia taking her elbow that oddly lessened the pain.

'Come, Contessa.' Claudia had picked up her bag. When they crossed the hall the woman tightened her hold. The staircase was wide and carpeted in a fine green and gold carpet that echoed the colour of the tiles in the hallway. Everything was so perfect; there was nothing to offend the eye.

Yet each step Alva took filled her with apprehension. They reached the first landing and Claudia escorted Alva to the left. There were many doors but the one the woman opened was the last one and faced down the corridor.

It was a huge room, not merely a bedroom but a sitting-room too. There was an antique writing desk; a scarlet silk covered chaise longue and the bed – a huge four-poster complete with scarlet bed hangings. The floors were wooden but here and there was an expensive Persian rug, cream and with dashes of scarlet. Going to the bed to test with a curious finger, the mattress for comfort, she saw, looking up, that these ceilings too were frescoed with scenes of barely clad nymphs and amorous shepherds. Had she liked that? Now it seemed to her to be a little too sensual for her taste. More brothel than palazzo, she thought, and she smiled a little: how did she know that about either place!

Claudia threw back the wooden shutters and the sunlight spilled into the room. She placed the suitcase on the bed and went to open another door that Alva saw, when she joined the woman, let on to a large bathroom. Alva went to inspect this, firstly looking at the ceiling in case there were any other scenes of an amorous nature. However here, there were none. The colour scheme was predominantly white, the bath, large and deep shone as if it were brand new. There was a walk-in shower and the fluffy rugs were in a variety of bright colours that softened the effect of the stark whiteness. The towels were coloured too, carefully chosen to match the rugs.

'It's all very beautiful,' Alva murmured.

'Oh yes, the bathroom is new, Contessa. The conte, he had all the plumbing renewed, it cost millions of lire I think but the conte said it had to be done. You remember the plumbing before,' Claudia laughed. 'Oh my, it groaned so in the night, do you remember, Contessa?' Then with a sympathetic nod Claudia said, 'Of course you do not, Contessa, but you will, one day it will all come back and you will remember so many good things.'

'Even groaning plumbing?' Alva managed a shy smile.

'Even that.'

The woman busied herself unpacking the meagre contents of Alva's case; Alva heard her clicking her tongue as she saw how poor the things were. Alva went out on to the wrought-iron balcony and saw the view that her maid had told her she loved. It was incredible. Down the slopes of olive groves, across the green vista, the sea could be seen, very blue and still. In fact the view itself was so still and calm it could have been a painting instead of reality. How strange that she did not recognize the view and saw it as if for the first time. It seemed impossible that such beauty had been obliterated from her mind. Yet something was there, a feeling inside her that made her just vaguely uncomfortable. It was beautiful and yet there was a *but* there, somewhere at the back of her mind.

Another maid came in, she carried a tray of tea things and there were small delicate cakes and tiny biscuits. Alva had eaten on the private jet that had flown her to the port but that was, she realized, some while ago. She sat at the small round table and poured the tea; it was as she liked it, quite weak; she did not take cream and there was none on the tray just a few slices of lemon. Someone had obviously remembered how she liked her tea. She took up a cake; it was sweet and delicate and melted on her tongue.

'Contessa,' Claudia said, 'come see, there are other clothes in the wardrobe, come look, you will wish to change perhaps. . . .' Claudia was trying to be kind but Alva could tell that the woman was appalled by her poor clothing. She went across and looked; there was an array of wonderful dresses in the deep, heavily carved wardrobe. The clothes were in all shades and hues and of fine silk and satin – there was a stack of soft cashmere sweaters in a myriad of jewelled colours and, in another closet, trousers and skirts and casual wear. As if aware of her mistress's curiosity, Claudia said, 'all this you left behind when you left. The conte did not throw it away, contessa.' And she nodded enthusiastically as if there was some hidden meaning behind that.

Alva smiled. 'Claudia, I will be glad to get out of this suit, I have it pinned at the waist, it's too big – I don't know why I have something that is so big.'

'I think you might have lost a little weight but not that much,' Claudia pursed her lips. 'Shall I run you a bath, Contessa? You liked a bath and with good oils too, which we have, you will feel better I think.'

'You're very kind, Claudia.'

'Not at all, it is my joy to serve you, Contessa!'

A thought came into her head that she could ask Claudia about this man, Antonio. This man with whom she was supposed to be friendly, yet she discounted the idea immediately. After all, it would be unfair to ask Claudia such a thing. She was employed by the conte and he might not like her questioning his servants. It might, as well, reflect badly on Claudia and cause her to lose her job. Better she found out herself, sometime . . . and sometime soon.

The jeans and lightweight pale-blue cashmere sweater fitted perfectly. It was a mystery why she would be wearing such an ill-fitting suit as she had when she left the hospital. Even if she had put on that many pounds during her separation, her weeks in the hospital would not have made it possible to lose so much weight. It had been weeks and not months that she had been confined to a hospital bed.

He came, as he had said, on time. Only an hour had passed since she had seen him in the hall, although it seemed longer. He cast a look at her, his eyes narrowing a little. Now her hair was loose, it was thick, straight hair, quite heavy and it moved across her cheeks as she walked. The shoulder-length bob flattered her finely sculptured features. She could look cool and aloof but she was like a diamond, fire and ice. Only you were not aware of the fire until you touched her, kissed her, lay with her. There was nothing cool in the way she had wrapped her body around him, offering up herself for his pleasure. These thoughts sent a scalding rush through him, awakening too many memories. These emotional feelings vied with anger. He stormed past her, going on to the balcony, gripping the wrought-iron rail and torturing the metal against his hands until he had control of himself. It was ridiculous to feel that way. When he had thought about her during their separation he had felt misery, anger and sometimes even fear, everything had eventually gone, fading away with time. Now and again he remembered the terrible thing she had done and the melancholy had returned. He had not thought he would ever feel desire again.

When he returned she was standing by the door, a puzzled expression on her face. Her dark green eyes were troubled, her full lips parted as if she would ask a question but seeing his expression, she closed her mouth and said nothing.

'I'm sorry,' he murmured. 'I had a need of air. Shall we go?'

'Of course.'

Although not a massive building, the palazzo was difficult to negotiate, for there were many corridors and different stairways. There were bedrooms situated over three floors, and six attic rooms; downstairs there was a library, a drawing-room and various other rooms of varying degrees of comfort. At the rear of the palazzo he led her into a beautiful sun lounge. It was full of light and colour and comfortable chairs. 'You did like to sit in here and read on winter days,' he murmured. 'If there is any sun, then you will find it here.' Opening the long glass doors she saw there was to the right of them, a loggia. It went around the house and would offer cool shade on hot days.

He took her outside; there were stables and she was not surprised when he told her that she rode quite well. She went and touched the horses and found she was not afraid of them but oddly familiar with their feel and smell.

Close to the palazzo there was an indoor swimming pool. The pool though was empty and when she asked why, he merely shrugged and said no one used it any more. 'Did I use it?' she asked.

'Yes, you were, are, a very athletic person. However you did prefer the outdoor pool. That is just along here and you will find that it has water – sea water actually.' Adjacent to the building that housed the drained swimming pool was a dilapidated building that marred the palazzo's perfection, like a flaw in a beautiful ornament. It had all the ornate features of the building that housed the swimming pool, but its windows were filthy and the roof tiles were in need of repair. Alva looked at her husband questioningly. 'I know,' he said, 'it's used for storage but I have to do something about it. *Sometime.*'

Everything else was beautiful, the setting, the mellow stone walls of the palazzo, the shady terraces where vines crawled up pillars and there were terracotta pots of gaudy geraniums and other colourful blooms set out in haphazard fashion on black and white mosaic floors.

The swimming pool area was laid with blue and white tiles, there were matching striped loungers and umbrellas and the water glinted dark blue in the sunshine.

'Even though there are two pools you used to like to drive down to the beach. It is not far, fifteen minutes and it is quite private. You enjoyed swimming there. You have a thing about the sea.'

'Yes, I think I can already feel that. It's quite beautiful, Conte.'

'Why so formal? You can call me Luca when we are alone.'

'I think we had better keep it formal,' she murmured. 'After all, I don't know you – at least the me that I am now doesn't. You're a stranger to me.'

'Of course,' he said in a clipped kind of way. She gave him a careful glance from beneath her long curling lashes. He was tall and well-built, more so than she had first thought. He was a muscular man but one, she imagined, without an ounce of fat. How had she captured such a man – she was not rich, could not have been to have arrived in such a poor state and if no one else had contacted her, or wanted to look after her. That was why she had had to come here. What did that make her? An orphan – she had to have had no family otherwise she would not be here as a last resort. She could have stayed in England. However, she had no money, no address and no one had been looking for her. If it had not been for a journalist with a long memory she might still have been there but seeing her photograph in the newspaper, he had gone into its archives, because something about her niggled at him. It was he who had found their wedding photographs; this was no poor little lost girl, she was the Contessa Mazareeze, estranged wife of the Conte Mazareeze of Santa Caterina island.

'May we sit?' she asked, seeing a carved stone bench by the lily pond.

'Yes, please do.'

'Sorry, I do feel a little weak.'

'Would you like me to fetch you something?'

'No, I'll be fine; really, it's just that this has been a long day.'

'Of course, perhaps we should not have walked so far.'

'Oh no, I love it, I like being outside. Being confined to a hospital room is not my idea of heaven. I haven't said, perhaps I should, it is very kind of you to have me come here. I'm sure I will get better more quickly by being here. It's so beautiful and peaceful and surely a place like this will stir my memory.'

'Perhaps it will. Anyway, what else could I do, Alva? You have no one else.'

'I don't? No one at all? Please tell me, Conte, I really know so little.'

'Well there is not much to tell. Your parents died when you were fourteen years old. They were working in India and were caught up in a cholera epidemic. . . .'

'India? Had they left me behind? Why were they there?' Curiosity caused a dark flush to invade her neck and cheeks. There was a look of animation and it really wounded him to see it there; however a kind of hope withered inside him, her memory would not be restored just because he told her who she was.

When he had first heard about her and her condition he had thought she was lying. His suspicions were aroused because he had just that week ordered his lawyer to contact her and ask for a divorce. It seemed far too convenient for her to have lost her memory. Yet seeing her now he realized she was not lying.

She might be able to fool the psychiatrist he had sent to examine her, but she could not fool him. There was something so vague about her and things were different about her that made him realize she was not deceiving him at all.

'As far as I know, they went to work at a hospital for the poor. Your father was a doctor and your mother was a nurse. They were very – I cannot think of the correct word in English – but perhaps compassionate will do? They gave their time to good causes when they could, and this opportunity came for them to be in India and so they went. You were at boarding school, I believe, so it wasn't a problem. I think they envisaged that in the long holiday you would go out there to be with them but it never happened. There was an aunt and you went to stay with her, I think she was on your mother's side, but it did not work out. She was not very kind to you, or so you said.'

Alva shot him a look as if suspecting he meant it as a criticism, but she folded her lips tightly together and said nothing.

'When you left school you went to university and there was no need for anyone to look after you. You studied politics and languages and after university you went to work for a politician. I had some business with him since he was something to do with trade and industry. That is how we met, at a meeting of delegates from your country and mine. You were with your boss because he could not speak Italian. He was an obnoxious fellow but it was a job, you said.'

She mused on what he had said for a long moment, she toed the ground, moving the tiny pieces of gravel about with her foot. Nothing of this came into her mind. No pictures of her kind and altruistic parents. Alva could not see herself at university, being a carefree student, nor in the exciting society of political power. Her memory bank was empty.

At length she asked. 'I wonder why he did not see me in the newspaper then, if I worked for him. It might have given him some good publicity.'

'Believe me, he would have been pleased to have been in the headlines. However, he disgraced himself over some affair or other and went to live abroad. The States I think.'

'Oh, really.'

'He was very unpopular with everyone. I should not be surprised if they had not set him up just to get rid of him.'

'Laws!'

'He rather liked you though. He thought you gave him class but that is something that you cannot get from someone else.'

She looked at him – *he* had class while *she* – well what was she? Well, hardly an honourable something or other.

'But the aunt did not come forward,' she murmured.

'Well, she probably wouldn't. I think she disliked you as much as I disliked the politician but for different reasons.'

'I wonder what those reasons were.'

'You were beautiful and clever and all the things she could not be. Also you married an Italian. I hardly think she approved of that.'

'How silly and spiteful that was. I mean leaving me there, not knowing anything, and having to trouble you.'

'It is no trouble, Alva. You are obviously not faking this illness.'

She turned furious eyes on him. 'Did you think that I was?'

He saw that she still had her essential spirit.

'I am afraid I rather suspected you might do something like that.'

Her expression was one of puzzlement, her brows pulled down, as she tried to visualize the woman she had been. She did not feel inside herself that she could fake this kind of thing but how did she know that she could not. It was impossible to know anything. Yet even if she had faked her illness, why would she? What benefit could she gain? They were parted; surely it had been an amicable parting.

'But why would I want to do that?' she asked.

He shrugged 'I don't know,' he murmured, yet instinctively

she knew that he was lying. He had meant what he said but now he wanted to back away from his statement. 'You might have wanted to forget . . . things.'

Alva shivered as a wind drifted by them; it caused the trees to rustle, yet it was a scented breeze. 'What things would I want to forget?'

Ignoring the question, he commanded, 'Come, you are cold, we should go back.'

'The clothes I came in?' she asked, deciding to let the matter of the *things* go for now.

'Your clothes were ruined in the accident. I offered to send some clothing to you but they said they would find you something to wear. That is why they are a bad fit.'

'Goodness, where was I living? I had to have some clothes, surely?'

'You had been staying at a flat that belonged to some friends who are abroad travelling. You do not remember where it was.'

She shivered again. She was not particularly cold, it was the way he had said that she would fake her illness that disturbed her more than anything else he said. That was the thing that stayed in her mind, teasing her. She hated the implication, yet she sensed, again from something deep inside her, that he would not be drawn on the matter. She would let it go, for now.

'What is that dome?' she pointed to a white dome peeping over the cypress trees.

'It is a summerhouse. You can see it tomorrow. Come, Alva, I should not like you to take cold.'

'All right.' She stood slowly. She looked up at him, he was so good-looking, and it was incredible that this man, who had everything, had chosen her to be his wife. 'I don't know how I can thank you, Conte, I really am so grateful.'

'It is the least I could do.' His reply was stiff and formal.

They turned to walk slowly back to the house. 'Renata is here but I doubt you will see her.'

'Renata?' she queried.

'My daughter.'

She stopped in her tracks, gazing up at him, puzzlement clouding her eyes.

He said at once. 'Not your daughter, Alva. Renata is my daughter by my first wife.'

'Oh, you had a previous wife? Before me I mean.'

'Yes I did. She was killed in a road accident. Renata was with her and has somehow never forgiven herself for being the one that lived.'

'How tragic,' she murmured, her heart filling with sympathy. 'The poor girl.'

'Well, yes, Renata has quite a few problems. I may as well tell you Alva, that you two never did get on.'

'Oh dear, we didn't? Was she jealous that you married me?'

He stiffened, pulling himself to his full height, his face set in haughty lines of barely concealed contempt. 'My daughter had been through a very bad time, Alva. Perhaps if you had been less critical you would have earned her respect.'

'I was critical of her to you?' she asked.

'Oh no, not to me. Alva, I do not think this is the time to discuss the pros and cons of anything.'

'Oh, but I do.' She stopped, standing looking up at him, not put off by his glacial expression. 'You seem to imply that I am some kind of monster stepmother.'

'I implied no such thing,' he said.

'I don't think I should stay here,' she whispered a hand now folded against her throat. 'Renata obviously has issues with me and I don't want to cause her unhappiness.'

'You won't. She won't be here; she's going back to university in the morning.'

'University? Then Renata is not a child?'

'No, she is nineteen.'

'So she was not a little child when I came here.'

'She was fifteen.'

'I see,' Alva murmured. A troubled teenage girl, only eight years her junior, no wonder they had had problems. She had hardly been in a position to understand and help a girl who was suffering so many traumas. She could see how difficulties would have arisen. This lifestyle would have been new to her, she would have been finding her way and it would have been testing even without a resentful teenage girl on the scene.

She looked up at the man she had married. His stare was cold and haughty; it seemed impossible to believe that they had been intimate with each other, that he had kissed her and trembled in her arms. Had he done that? Perhaps it had been a cold marriage, yet instinctively she knew it could not have been. She was not a cold person. As she tried to imagine what it would have been like, she felt a faint stirring of pleasure deep inside her. Hastily she looked away from him.

'I think I need to rest,' she murmured.

'Of course, I'll take you back to the house.

CHAPTER TWO

ALVA wakened early. She sat up in bed, running her hands up to her temples and massaging the flesh, trying to remember ... *something, anything*. For a moment she felt confused, uncertain as to where she was. Struggling out of the tangle of bedding and leaving the bed, she went to the window, throwing back the wooden shutters to look out on a scene of misty whiteness.

Thin streaks of sunbeams speared the pale mist that clung to the tops of the trees. Everything was glistening damply. There was the sound of birds but little else, just above the swirling mist she could see the very blue ocean. Of course, it was Santa Caterina. She was staying with her husband, Conte Mazareeze.

The view was so perfect and yet somehow, deep inside her, there was a feeling of – what was it? She sought to describe it – *discontent?* She shrugged the thought aside; the feeling came from her momentary confusion and nothing more.

Turning from the window she saw her cast-off clothing and without thought, she pulled on the jeans and the cashmere sweater. She had to get out. The room seemed to stifle her, the scarlet and green, the overripe maidens and cherubs on the ceiling were too sensual and, at the same time, suffocating.

The house was silent; she passed through it quietly. From

somewhere she could smell the delicious aroma of fresh bread and coffee. Her stomach gurgled a little with pleasure but ignoring it, she flung back the great door and stepped on to the tiled terrace.

She headed swiftly for the domed building she had seen yesterday. Reaching it, she saw it was as the conte had told her, a summerhouse – a classical, white portico building, quite exquisite. She peered inside through the glass doors; it was furnished with the kind of furniture that would not have disgraced a sitting-room. Trying the door she found it locked. There was something about this spot that awakened an alien feeling inside her. She could not comprehend what kind of feeling it was, was it fear? Or was it sadness? She could not sort out in her mind how she felt, but that she felt something was evident. Her spine felt as if cold fingers were running along the bones.

It made no sense and yet she wanted to run away from the place.

Spying a path running to the back of the building she ran towards it, taking it at a fast pace, wanting to get away from the summerhouse and whatever it was that had once happened there to make her feel so strange.

The path twisted through a copse of trees, spiralling downwards. Eventually after about a mile, she came to a wrought-iron gate. She opened the gate and found herself on a rutted road. The road was steep but she took the downward slope. On one side of the road were olive groves and on the other was the high, honey-coloured stone wall that encircled, she assumed, the palazzo.

Unsure of where she was going and what she was doing, she nevertheless followed the road as it twisted and turned. The walls of the palazzo were gone now and in its place were vineyards. The waves of white mist drifted by her like a wraith, yet never obscured the way.

At last the road levelled out; the first red-roofed house appeared and then another and another, until at last there was a cluster of houses, the road became a cobbled street and she found herself in a small village of brightly painted houses. There were passages between the houses – some were broad cobbled steps – but she kept to the main road. Eventually the road opened up and she found herself in a square. There was a church, a baker, a bar and a shop that appeared to be a general store.

Four men were sitting at a table outside the bar. They had cups of coffee and had been chatting loudly when she first came into the square then, seeing Alva, they stopped talking and stared at her.

After hesitating, she walked on, as she neared them she murmured, '*Buon giorno*.'

To her surprise, the men stood – three were wearing caps and these they removed, bowing their heads lightly. '*Buon giorno*, Contessa,' they said.

Nervously she smiled, and then hurriedly crossed the square. She needed sanctuary – wanted to be alone, to think. What had she done? Was she running away? She could not think what had made her follow the road, what impulse had driven her to do something so foolish. It had not occurred to her that people would know who she was, that it would be impossible for her to remain anonymous. She looked different from the Caterinians, being so fair. She ought to have realized she would stand out.

The church door was open. Running up the steps she went inside, sliding into a pew at the back. The interior was beautiful, rich with gold and with incredibly vibrant frescoes.

As her eyes became accustomed to the surroundings she noted that there were several women kneeling in the front pews, their heads covered. Perhaps she and Luca had married in this very church. Luca, how the name tripped from her tongue. Yesterday he had been the conte and now in her mind he had become Luca and it had happened so naturally, as if she had never lost her memory of him. Yet as she pursued him further in her mind, nothing came to the fore. Just his name, Luca; she murmured it out loud as if this would trigger something but it did not, yet it sounded so sweet on her tongue and with it came a rush of feeling so potent it knocked the very breath from her body.

Her stomach grumbled. It had been so foolish to come all this way without eating something. Yesterday she had not gone down to dinner and had sent word that she was going to bed early. She had eaten nothing but a couple of biscuits and now she had walked at least four miles. Having no purse with her, she knew she would have to walk back to the palazzo and up hill all the way, on an empty stomach.

When she left the church the sun had dominance, it beat down on the shiny surface of the square. The men were still outside the bar; a man near the general store was swilling down the area in front of the shop with a bucket of water.

The sound of a car's engine caused her to pause before crossing the square. The car, a low-slung white two-seater sporty model, pulled up suddenly and the door opened to reveal Luca.

With restrained elegance he pulled himself from the car and crossed to her side. 'Alva,' he murmured, 'get in.' Although he spoke softly, there was a command in his voice. She looked up at him, thought of saying she preferred to walk, but then realized that would be foolish. Her legs felt rather like a young foal's and twice as unsteady. Gratefully, she slid into the passenger seat as he opened the door. Without looking at her, he slammed the door to close it; the noise of it seemed to echo around the square.

As he drove past the bar, she saw the men watching their progress with interest. Turning she looked at Luca. He was looking stern and uncompromising. Obviously he was annoyed with her.

'How did you know where I was?' she asked.

'A telephone call.'

She clicked her tongue impatiently. 'There was no need for that. Why would anyone do that anyway?'

'Because they know you are not, shall I say, yourself, and they are concerned. You wander in the square at seven a.m. and you think it will not cause comment. *Dio mio* you must be mad if you think that!'

'Well I am mad, in a way, isn't that so?'

'If you like.'

Her stomach swelled yet not from hunger, there was a dull pain there and she could not explain it to herself. He was after all only agreeing with her and what did she expect? That he would understand her confusion.

'You really don't like me very much do you?' She dared, even though she dreaded the confirmation.

He said after a while. '*Va bene*.'

'What did I do to make you dislike me?' She dared the question, yet dreaded the reply.

'Now is not the time for this,' he said sternly. His hands moved confidently across the steering wheel. They were capable, strong hands, darkly tanned. She thought of them touching her body and gave a little gasp. He turned to give her a quick glance.

'What is it?'

'Nothing, I think I should know everything. It's cruel to be this way and not to tell me the reason.'

'Being what way, Alva? Have I been rude to you? Have I made you uncomfortable?'

'Of course not, you are almost too polite.' Then looking at him she added, 'Frigidly so.'

'I am sorry; I cannot help how I feel, Alva.'

His apology made her feel suddenly sad; it was possible that she had done something unforgivable and it troubled her. That in itself did not really make sense, for surely if she had done something so bad that her husband no longer loved her, then it followed that she would not care. But she did care, cared too much for her own peace of mind.

'Did you love me?' she asked.

'Love you?' He rasped out the question, his jaw was set firm. 'What is love?'

'Deep feelings for another person, emotional involvement, a willingness to do anything to make that person happy, putting them before yourself,' she shrugged. 'Something like that I would imagine.'

'Emotional involvement?' he reflected on the words, saying them softly, almost under his breath. When he next said something she knew it was meant as a rebuttal of any feelings of love she might suspect him of once having. It was also meant as an insult. 'The sex was good.'

She waited a moment, the car now turned into the gates. 'I'm pleased I was able to get something right.'

He made a slight hiss as he took a deep breath. So, he was not expecting that. Perhaps the other Alva had never spoken up to him, was it possible she had been a doormat and then for some reason done something reprehensible? It could be that the reprehensible act had been a cry for help. She had only his word that she had been bad, it could be that she was not bad in other people's eyes. Claudia seemed to respect and like her, so obviously she had been good to her maid. Yet Alva knew she could not ask anything of Claudia, it would not be fair on the woman and it would not be the done thing anyway.

The car drew to a stop outside the entrance to the palazzo, Luca got out and she waited until he had gone around the front and opened the door for her. As elegantly as she could, she swung her legs around and climbed out of the car. There was a little frisson of pleasure as she realized she had left the car with style. As she passed him, for he stood still holding the door like a smart chauffeur, her sleeve brushed his arm. He recoiled from her as if she had stuck a needle in his arm. Alva looked up at him, staring into his haughty handsome face, his dark-golden coloured eyes met her gaze and he made no attempt to avert his eyes from her scrutiny.

'I must have been a real bitch,' she said.

'I would not use that word,' he said.

'You wouldn't?'

'Definitely not, Alva. You were difficult, you made things difficult but there was nothing bitchy in what you did.'

Her stomach heaved, she felt the urge to be sick, felt an acrid taste crawl up her throat.

'Excuse me,' she said and then she turned and ran away. She reached the bathroom; her stomach had to be empty but nevertheless something came gushing from her mouth. Waves of dizziness came over her and she sank on to the cool tiles, resting her cheek against the coldness, longing for the vertigo and the pain to go away.

It was Claudia who came and found her, helping her up, pushing aside her apologies with kind words. Soon Alva was lying on the bed, a cool damp towel over her eyes and forehead. Her eyes closed, she felt herself drifting away into nothingness.

Later, perhaps an hour had passed, when Claudia came with a tray of tea and warm rolls, urging Alva to eat a little.

'I forgot about my medication, Claudia, in my bag. Would you please. . . ?'

'A moment, Contessa.' The woman moved confidently across the room and retrieved Alva's handbag from the wardrobe.

Alva took the cocktail of tablets. Perhaps that was what had made her feel so ill, yet she knew that could not be the reason for her nausea. The medication had not had any effect on her before. Besides, she was nearly finished with taking them. The doctor had given her just enough and once they were finished she was to try to get by without them.

'Eat a little,' Claudia urged.

Alva did so, her stomach yawning even more emptily and, surprisingly, after the second bite, she found that the food slid down easily. The rolls were delicious and the tea hot and weak, as she liked it.

Claudia came later and ran a bath for her. It all seemed a little strange to have someone do these tasks for her. She was certain it was not how she had been brought up. Obviously, she had to have been independent, being away at school and then living with an unpleasant aunt. Her aunt, if she disliked her so much, was unlikely to have fussed around her.

'Claudia, what was I like . . . *before*?' Curiosity got the better of her, the words slipping out when the woman came and said that her bath was ready.

'Why, Contessa, just like now, *gentile*, Contessa, *simpatico*.'

Claudia smiled, her head to one side, as if she thought that Alva was crazy for asking the question. 'You will not change your character, Contessa, just because you cannot remember. How can you do such a thing?'

'Maybe,' Alva murmured.

She crossed the room towards the bathroom. Claudia put her hands on her hips.

'The *signorina*,' she shook her head despairingly. 'But I must not say – except – she is not *simpatico*.'

Alva went into the bathroom, closing the door behind her. She dare not go there with Claudia. Of course, Alva knew that the woman was referring to Renata, the girl to whom supposedly Alva was unkind. Glancing at herself in the mirror she saw that she looked pale and sickly still. She examined herself not out of vanity but of a wish to try to understand who she was. Was she really the archetypical wicked stepmother or was there more to Renata than her father saw? She would never find out – not only would she not see Renata apparently, but Luca thought his daughter above suspicion. She had not handled the relationship with her stepdaughter very well. It had to have been difficult for them both, but as the more mature woman she should have perhaps tried harder.

'I don't feel I'm a spiteful person. I'm not a bitch, he said that.'

She lay in the tub, Claudia had tipped a generous amount of bath foam and the bubbles were abundant and deliciously sweet. She rested her head and enjoyed the experience.

Eventually leaving the bath, she wrapped herself in a large soft towel, and then went to lie on the bed.

Hearing the door open, expecting Claudia, she turned her head and saw to her dismay that it was not Claudia but that it was Luca.

'I heard you were ill,' he said sternly.

'I'm all right,' she murmured.

'I think we should call the doctor,' he insisted, moving deeper into the bedroom.

'Do you need assurance that I am not faking.'

'I think we already established, Alva, that you are not faking, but you are obviously not well, Alva, and I would be happy if the doctor came to check you over.'

'Very well,' she agreed, before turning away from him.

He closed the door; she turned to make sure he had gone through it. Of course it was obvious that everything she did or would do would be reported to him. He had to have set the servants to spy on her – and was Claudia also part of the conspiracy? She realized that she had better be careful what she said and of what questions she asked.

In spite of knowing that the doctor would come to visit, she decided to dress.

The strength had returned to her limbs and now that she had eaten something and bathed, she felt quite refreshed. From the chest of drawers she took some underwear, it was silky and flimsy and there were many brassieres and panties in a variety of colours. She chose a lavender set and then from the closet, she took out a linen skirt with a matching top in a delicious shade of deep pink. Looking at herself when dressed she realized she had chosen well. The vivid pink suited her pale complexion and her sleek blonde hair. She had her make-up bag with her and she took out a lipstick that would not clash with the colour of her outfit, slicked it over her lips and then, after fluffing out her bobbed hair, went to look for a pair of shoes. There were lots of shoes. Was she a spendthrift? It certainly looked as if she was a woman who could shop with a vengeance. There was a pair of strappy white sandals with a slim not-too-high heel, and she slipped her feet into them.

There was no one about when she went downstairs. She remembered the sun lounge, the place that Luca had said she liked, and so she made her way there. Someone was there already, a dark, very slender girl. She was not quite beautiful but had perfectly formed features and a fine aristocratic bone structure. Her nose was not as large as her father's and her eyes were the colour of dark, rich chocolate. Alva guessed that she was Renata Mazareeze, her stepdaughter.

The girl was exquisitely dressed, having that strong sense of style that many Italians had. The way she wore a silk scarf at her neck, the casual way the cuff on her satin blouse was turned, the well-cut black trousers, all looked expensive but worn with aplomb.

The girl said before Alva could speak, 'I didn't want to see you. Weren't you told that?' She spoke in a rude tone of voice. Obviously, the girl had no idea about good manners. She looked such a well-bred girl but Alva realized that appearance could be deceptive, and it certainly was as far as her stepdaughter was concerned.

'Yes, Renata I was told that. However, your father told me that I liked to sit in this room. I was not following you nor was I looking for you. I'm just looking for somewhere to sit and pass the time.'

'Why don't you sit and pass the time in London?'

'I don't know,' Alva said. She crossed the room and took the pale cream armchair.

'Your father invited me here until I get well.'

'Get well!' The girl scoffed. 'As if you are really ill. Don't think I believe your story, Alva, I know why you're here. You lost your pampered lifestyle and you want it back.'

'If you say so, Renata,' Alva said smoothly.

'You'll give yourself away, Alva. You aren't that clever.'

'Renata, you are a lovely young girl and you are obviously very clever, so why do you waste so much energy hating me?'

The girl stared at her as if the question had somehow confused her. Alva allowed herself to meet the gaze of her stepdaughter and at the same time, to try to drive away the misery that was there inside her. For this young girl to feel such passionate dislike must mean that it was in some way warranted. It could not just be that Renata was jealous that her father had married another woman. It could not be that simple.

'You know why and you know what you did to my father; don't pretend you don't remember because *I* will never believe it. You cannot forget something so bad.' The girl stared at Alva, her eyes spewing out such raw hatred that Alva shivered.

However, managing to maintain a cool exterior she said, 'That's up to you, Renata. But I *am* telling the truth and if you want me to feel really remorseful then you should tell me what I did that was so bad.'

'What you did?' Renata asked. 'You want me to say it. You did lots of things. You were horrid to me.' She took a breath and waited for a long moment, as if expecting Alva to deny it. 'You flirted with men – probably you did even more than flirt only I could never prove that – but that's not all, the most unspeakable thing you did was to—'

'*Renata*!'

The voice whipped across the room. The girl turned around to meet the furious gaze of her father.

'The helicopter has returned. Do you have your things ready?'

'Why don't you tell her, Papa? Tell her what she did and then you'll see how she's lying. She's so good at lying, Papa, you know that.'

'Do you have your things, Renata?' He repeated the question. He was so cold, Alva thought, that he made her shiver. After defying her father by holding his gaze in the end Renata shrugged.

'I won't be long!'

'Don't be, Antonio will fly us to Roma but I must be back here for a meeting.'

'Very well, Papa, give me ten minutes.' The girl swept out, dramatically slamming the door behind her.

Alva started at the echoing sound but then sought to gain her composure.

'You must not pay any attention to Renata, she is young,' he shrugged, as if age excused bad manners.

Alva wanted to say something, to let him know how she felt but she managed with effort to say nothing.

'The doctor is here. I will send him to you. He will stay for lunch and then Guido will take him to the port and he will take the ferry back to the mainland.'

The idea of having lunch with a stranger, and a doctor at

that, filled Alva with apprehension but again she said nothing. Obviously, the doctor had come from the mainland and so she could hardly send him back without some sustenance.

'There is a ferry, to and from the mainland?'

'Of course there is, Alva, but it would not be polite to send him back without lunch.'

'Of course not, I was not meaning to suggest I do that, I was just curious.'

'There are two ferries a day and that is all. The first is in the early morning and then there is one at three o clock. The last ferry leaves the mainland at 7 p.m. winter and summer. However, if you should wish to go then Antonio will take you in the launch.'

'Antonio seems to do everything,' she murmured.

'Yes, he does.'

She wondered what this paragon was actually like – was he young and handsome or more mature? She recalled that the conte had said she had liked him, had she liked him too much? Was he one of the men she had flirted with? The thoughts tormented her – each one led her nowhere, just to a dark place where there was no past and seemed also to be no future.

'Will you see Doctor Martino here?'

'Yes, if that's all right.'

'He may wish to examine you,' Luca suggested.

'Then I will make other arrangements.'

'As you wish. *A piu tardi.*'

'*Arriverderci!*'

Doctor Martino was a man in his sixties with a shock of white hair. He had a kind face and at once Alva realized he was someone that she could relate to. He came and sat opposite her and launched into a warm explanation of who he was, that he had known her when she had first come as a bride and that he had treated her previously. He was very efficient and explained that he had already been in touch with the hospital in London to have access to her medical records.

He had only that morning spoken to her consultant after the conte had told him she had been ill, and was quite familiar now with the nature of her complaint.

'Thank you,' Alva murmured. 'I think the conte worried unnecessarily. I'm afraid I had been rather silly. I walked to the village without eating anything this morning. I, well, I had a difference of opinion, sort of, with the conte and I think that upset me. In other words, maybe it was emotional rather than physical.'

'Perhaps, but let me take your temperature and we will see.' He popped a thermometer into her mouth and chatted generally while he waited for the mercury to rise or fall. When he checked it he murmured and nodded appreciatively.

'Your temperature is a little under, Contessa, but it is nothing to worry about. You are bound to have your ups and downs; you were involved in a serious accident. Although your physical wounds have healed, the shock will take some time, even if you were able to remember. Tell me, Contessa, when you came out of the coma you had no idea who you were? Not the slightest inkling?'

'No, I looked at a blank wall. There was nothing.'

'And your consultant tells me there was no concussion, so that is a blessing. You know it is possible, Contessa, that you will never remember anything.'

'I'm praying that isn't going to be the case, Doctor Martino, but yes, I have had that explained to me.'

When he had finished, she ordered them tea and when one of the servants brought it, Alva suggested they go and sit in the loggia. It was deliciously warm now and she had an urge to be outside. It was something she thought that she liked.

'That will be pleasant, Contessa.'

'Please can you not call me, Alva?' she implored. 'I don't feel like a contessa!'

'I would like that, Alva. You would have me call you Alva before you went away, you know.'

'Well, that's something that hasn't changed about me.'

'I don't imagine very much has changed about you, Alva. You are as beautiful as always.'

'Thank you,' she smiled up at him, accepting the compliment with grace.

They settled themselves in comfortable chairs on the loggia. At the far side there was a fountain of pale marble featuring slender nymphs draining their water jars into the shell-like shape of the base. She enjoyed the gentle tinkle of the music and the smell radiating from the pots of colourful blooms. Alva poured the tea and while she did the doctor, without her asking, told her the history of Santa Caterina.

He was very knowledgeable and made it interesting. Apparently the Mazareeze had been masters of the island for centuries, although it was suspected that they had once been rogues *before* they were aristocrats! She found that amusing, that the haughty conte and his family could be descendants of some ne'er-do-wells, even if it was in the long ago past. It certainly gave him a touch of humanity.

Yet for all that, they were good masters and fair to their employees, no matter how humble. Olive trees were a source of income, as well as acres of vineyards. The climate was perfect all the year round and they were not subjected to the intense heat or the cold winters that were prevalent on the mainland. Crops of tomatoes flourished, as did lemon trees and various vegetables. The farmers had shares in their crops and much profit was ploughed back into the island.

The small resort where Alva had disembarked had been developed from a small fishing village, and now boasted a marina and an exclusive hotel. Many of the townsfolk also ran *pensions* from their own homes; these catered for those who preferred a more authentic stay on Santa Caterina. Several rather exclusive designer outlets had opened in the town, although they closed from late autumn to early spring. Not many ventured to the island in the winter months, although it would be possible to have an enjoyable time. The conte preferred to have moments of peace and rest for his people and for himself.

'He runs it all?' Alva asked, somewhat amazed.

'Oh yes. He has assistants, of course, but he does not lock himself away. If anyone wants to see him with complaints or plans or ideas, then he is available to them. The conte is well respected and I might add, Alva, he is loved too. His father practically left Luca bankrupt but Luca is a different man from him. He has worked very hard to make everything profitable. We are finally getting somewhere.'

'Really?' That cold haughty man was loved – that seemed rather amazing. She could not imagine him being sufficiently thawed for anyone to want to love him.

'You know a good deal, Doctor Martino.'

'Please, Alfredo, and yes, Alva I do. You see I grew up here. My father was a *paesano*, but I had, from who knows where, some ability, and so Luca's grandfather paid for me to go to university. It is thanks to him I am now what I am.'

The day went well for Alva. She felt better for the first time that she had been at the palazzo. Alfredo confirmed that there was nothing really physically wrong with her – the incident when she had been sick, had been probably caused by over-exercising before food. She rather thought it was brought on by her wrangling with Luca but she did not want to go into great detail. It was too personal.

They ate lunch on the loggia; she enjoyed the food too, a salad and pasta and delicious ice cream that was made on the island. She took a small glass of wine, not one from Luca's vineyards but a fine Chianti that Claudia brought out with their meal. Obviously it had been chosen because it had been remembered that she particularly liked it.

Later they strolled in the grounds and ended up at the summerhouse. Alfredo said.

'You know, Alva, when you left you had been through a bad time. It could be that you had not overcome that. Of course, you do not remember . . . *anything*?'

'No, nothing, everything is a blank, as I said.'

'Yes, yes, Alva, I do not doubt you but you never know, some little trigger might have made you aware of something. Losing a baby is. . . .'

'What?' She stopped, taking hold of the doctor's arm. 'I lost a baby?'

'Alva, I am so sorry, I thought the conte would have said something.'

'He's told me nothing!' She starred up into Alfredo's kind brown eyes. 'What happened? Did I go full term, was I. . . ?'

'Alva, let us sit in the summerhouse, come. . . .'

After the doctor had left Alva, longing to be alone, went outside and down the path to the summerhouse. There was something that she could not identify but which kept drawing her to the place.

It was blissfully warm and she went and sat outside on the steps that led to the tiny terrace. The evening shadows crept over the trees, a warm soft dusk, and the tips of the trees seemed to be on fire as the sun spread scarlet fingers over the horizon.

The revelation that she had lost her baby had shaken her. It had been difficult maintaining her composure in front of the doctor, yet she had somehow managed to do so. It was the way to glean even more information, for had she given way to how she really felt, she was certain he would not have gone into as much detail.

She had been six months pregnant and she had nearly died. There were complications for she had fallen down the stairs. Although the stairs now had a green and gold exquisite carpet, at that time the marble surface had been uncovered. She had bounced like a ball from the top to the bottom.

It had been, Doctor Martino told her, a difficult pregnancy anyway, she had been ill for most of the time. It was a dreadfully hot summer too which had not helped.

She had to be accident prone, falling down the stairs and then, after she had left Luca, being knocked down by a driver who had not even had the decency to stop.

Spreading her fingers across her stomach she tried to conjure up what it had felt like, Luca's child growing inside her. Was he not happy that she was pregnant?

He had told her when she asked about their relationship, that the sex had been good. That did not equate well with a loving partnership, the beginning of two people starting a family. Perhaps he had not wanted a child, after all, he had Renata.

Or was that why he no longer even liked her? Was it because she had lost his child in a terrible accident? *Did he blame her for that?* Yet how on earth could she be to blame? She would not have fallen down the stairs on purpose; she might have lost her memory but she knew in her mind that she would never have done that. She was too much of a coward anyway and her vivid imagination, as it did now, would surely then have conjured up for her all the things that could have gone wrong. She could have damaged her spine, her head, broken her body beyond repair. The prospect of what could have happened caused her to shudder violently.

She wrapped her arms around her legs and, bending her back, rested her head on her folded knees. The scent of the garden was more intense now and the very air seemed to grow warmer, even with the imminent departure of the sun. She felt a terrible sadness growing in her. It settled inside her, deep at the very pit of her. It ached like an intense physical pain and caused a moan-like sigh to escape her.

'So you are here.' The voice wafted to her, seeming to come from a long way off, but when she raised her head and opened her eyes, she saw that Luca was no more than two feet away from her.

'People have been calling you, did you not hear?'

She said. 'If I had heard them I would have answered. I'm not trying to be melodramatic.'

'No one said you were, Alva. Dinner is almost ready and we have guests.'

She looked up at him and felt something inside her, a kind of fury that she could no longer be bothered to control. This physically attractive man had the power to arouse such passion inside her.

'I don't do guests,' she snapped the words at him. 'I don't know who I am – how can I talk to your guests? I'm here because I have no where else to go, so don't include me in your social life!'

'That's rather a self-pitying statement, Alva, even for you.'

'Damn you Luca, just stop this now! You don't want me here so let me go and stop drip-feeding me your hatred. I don't know what I did, what I was capable of; I can't answer or excuse anything. I just want to be left on my own.'

'Do not be silly, Alva; the best way to get over this is to mix with people. They may trigger your memory.'

'I don't believe that. If anything were going to trigger my memory it would surely be the fact that I lost my baby. I can't even remember that, Luca, so don't tell me mundane things like guests for dinner will do me good.'

He had gone very pale. Even in the blue twilight she could see. His hands clenched at his sides and his lips thinned.

'I did not know you had been told that, Alva. I wanted to tell you that myself.'

'Oh yes, and when would that be? I've been here two days and I've had no mention of it from you.'

'It has hardly been appropriate. Should I have told you the moment you arrived? Or earlier today when things were going on in my life from which I could not escape? I wanted to be able to spend time with you, to talk about it.'

She flicked her tongue over her lips, feeling uncomfortably guilty now. He was obviously telling the truth, she did not think he would lie about such a thing. He had lost his baby too; she had not given any consideration to that fact.

She stood, smoothing down her skirt. 'Well, I know now,' she murmured.

'Alva, I have to have dinner with these people, perhaps we could talk later.'

'I don't know, what is there to say?'

He stared at her, the momentary compassion gone from his face, now he was that cold and haughty man once more, barely approachable. Still she relented; she had to give him the opportunity to say something about the loss of their child.

'Perhaps we should talk,' Alva said. 'But tomorrow, if you have time.'

'I will make time. Will you come back to the house? Perhaps you would like a little dinner in your room?'

'Maybe a sandwich or something, I had lunch with Doctor Martino.'

However, she let him escort her back to the house. She was only conscious of his hand cupping her elbow when it was no longer there. He let her go as they entered the hall. From somewhere she could hear laughter, a woman's tinkling laugh and then the rumble of a man's. It seemed so inappropriate that people should be laughing just then. Turning she looked up at Luca and he nodded his head, as if he agreed.

*

The next morning she found some lightweight casual trousers and a pale green and white chequered shirt. Last evening, after eating some cheese and bread she had slept deeply. She knew the tablets she was on aided her sleep pattern, but even so it was, oddly, the best sleep she had had in a long time.

Claudia brought her breakfast of warm rolls and butter and coffee. She relayed the information that the conte's guests had left by the launch at eight o clock. 'I had not realized they stayed the night,' Alva murmured, more to herself than to Claudia.

'*Sí*, Contessa, Signor Paolo and Signora Sophia have their own rooms. Ah, Contessa.' Claudia hit herself lightly on the forehead. '*Scusi* – Signor Paolo is the brother of the conte – the younger one.'

'I see.' That was why he had wanted her to join them at dinner. She had thought from what he had said, that the people that were dining with him were business acquaintances, she had not realized they were family. She was momentarily mortified by her rudeness, and then thought she had no reason to feel so guilty. After all, Luca had not told her that it was family who were guests. Yet would she have changed her mind? She doubted her ability to meet people just yet; it was hard enough getting by day by day living in this black fog without pretending that all was normal.

'And the conte says, Contessa, that he will meet you in the sun lounge at ten-thirty. He has had to go to one of the farms but he will be back.'

'Thank you, Claudia. I'll be waiting for him,' she smiled at the woman. Claudia was the only person who made her feel halfway normal.

Alva went out on to the loggia, it was pleasantly warm, the soft scents of morning wafted to her in an easy breeze; there was the scent of lemon and pine and a stronger perfume that she thought might be jasmine. She walked the length of the loggia, feeling restless and confused. How cruel that she could not remember anything about this perfect place. It was lovely, it appealed to her, yet she could not remember one single aspect of her life here. Had she ever been happy and in love, a new bride looking forward to a long and fulfilled life with the man she loved? Perhaps she would never remember!

An hour sped by, during which time Alva became more irritable. Luca had not materialized, probably he had no intention of doing so. He had more important things to do than to discuss things with her, even though the discussion concerned the loss of their child!

Angry now, she left the loggia and took a route that led to the stables. There were a couple of boys there cleaning out. With an imperious manner, that she adopted in case there were questions, she asked that they saddle a horse for her. There was no hint of a refusal and they hurried to do her bidding. They saddled up Star, a chestnut mare, not more than fourteen hands, that seemed placid enough. Without difficultly or hesitation, Alva mounted, tapped her heels into Star's sides, and guided the reins urging the mare to the left. They trotted down the drive where she had come in the car and once she reached the lodge, she urged the horse through. She took a left turn, riding away from town; there was what looked like a bridleway about a mile on and she took that. It was so peaceful and quiet, just her and the horse and she felt a sudden rush of real pleasure. This was something she really enjoyed, she recognized the feeling. It was the first taste of joy she had had since arriving in Italy.

The bridleway widened; on either side now there were pine trees and here and there grassy dunes. Eventually, the blue sea came into view and she found herself down on the beach. It was a narrow strip of beach about three miles in length. Just north of a large sand dune there was a decaying grey tower. Perhaps it was a watch tower or gun emplacement – whatever, it was crumbling into nothing. It was out of place here yet it seemed familiar, as if she had been there, resting against its wall. It had to be fanciful imagining. How could she remember that old thing and not the man that she had married! More to the point, just why a building should trigger something in her head when she could not remember the agony of losing her unborn child, confirmed that she was imagining it. Stilling the horse, she slid from its back and, holding the reins, went up to the building.

The walls were more solid than she had first realized, although part of the wall had fallen down, as if it had been pounded by a storm. Peering inside, she saw it was quite narrow but there was a flight of stairs which twisted at the middle, spiralling down, but it was too dark for her to see how far they went. Where could they lead? She recalled Alfredo telling her of the piratical past of Luca's ancestors – could it be that the stairs led to an underground passage that led beyond the walls of the palazzo? The very structure was visible from the sea so it was not really secret. Everyone would know where it was. If raiding parties came it would suit *their* purpose to use that to get into the palazzo. If indeed that was where the stairs led.

Star whinnied, crying for her attention; she was stamping her feet as if anxious for a run along the shore. 'OK,' she said. 'I will let you have your own way, but I have to find out about this structure.'

Mounting the horse, she gave Star her head and they cantered along the flat hard sand until they came to a rocky inlet. She turned the horse around and went back the other way, now and again cantering through the soft white tipped waves. After a couple of rides up and down and beach, she slowed Star and dismounted. Kicking off her shoes she waded into the sea. It was warm to her feet and with a sudden rush of rashness, she pulled off her jeans and sweater, throwing them over Star's saddle, she waded into the foamy waves, until they brushed her waist, now she glided through them, breaking out into a steady crawl and feeling again that sense of elation that she had felt while riding Star. There was a pure sensual delight to be found in these physical pursuits. It made her glad to know, too, that she was not a weakling that she enjoyed physical exercise – even more, that she relished it.

At last satiated and happy, she turned and made to leave the sea, her silken underwear clinging to her slender curves. It was only as the water reached her knees that looking at where she had left Star she saw the horse was not there.

Panicking, she ran from the sea, holding her hand up to shade her eyes she looked along the beach but the horse was nowhere to be seen, nor were her clothes. Wherever the horse had gone she had gone with her clothes still across the saddle. Obviously, the mare had not galloped or the clothes would be on the sand. Alva ran up the beach quickly, heading to where the path was that she had taken.

Star was there but the horse was not alone. A large black stallion was keeping her company and standing holding on to the reins of both horses was Luca. His eyes raked her from the top of her sea-sodden hair to the tip of her pink-painted toenails and, lingering on the journey, over the curves of her body. She would not look down at herself and she did not realize that the thin silk left nothing whatsoever to the imagination.

'What do you think you are doing?' he asked, imperious and yet oddly angry.

'Swimming,' she answered pertly.

'I know that. But in that—' He brushed a hand in her direction.

'You said it was a private beach.' Yet had he said that? She was not certain that he had ever said anything about the beach; it was Claudia with whom she had talked about the beach but perhaps no one had said it was private, maybe she had *remembered* it was.

'Does that make it any better?' he asked.

'Of course it does. Anyway I do have something on, and I'm not exactly nude.'

'Aren't you?' he asked darkly, raising an eyebrow.

He released the reins on the horses, taking her clothes that, remarkably, were still on Star's saddle. The horses moved away towards some grassy plants on the small dune.

She had the urge to tuck her hands across herself; there was something in his look, a kind of proprietary insolence that made her tremble, but if she did that she had the feeling that he would have won. Instead of behaving modestly, she opted for the bold, holding his gaze and letting her hands relax at her sides.

'We don't have a towel,' he said.

'*We* don't,' she said, trying to keep it light. 'But if you will excuse me, I'll get dressed in that dune,' she nodded her head. Silently he handed her clothes to her. Turning, she ran up the dune and down the other side. The sun was up now and it was deliciously warm in the shelter of the huge sand hill. She peeled off her silk underwear and then slipped into the trousers and shirt.

She left the shelter of the dune, running down with more energy than she had experienced for some while. He was still there, his long-fingered hand caressing her horse. 'I believe we had a meeting arranged,' he said, handing her the reins of the horse.

'You were late. I was tired of waiting.'

'I had important business to attend to. You can't always gauge how long these things will take.'

'Something that was more important than talking to me

about our dead baby?' She taunted recklessly.

He stared back at her now, raising a brow, his appraisal was damning. She knew she was behaving badly yet something inside her was demanding that she cause some kind of reaction from him. She needed him to lose his cool, to be emotional, to show some kind of feeling even if that feeling were anger. Yet why did she need this? He was nothing to her. But if the conte *was* nothing, why did he stir up all these wild emotions?

'Alva,' he said sternly.

'What?'

She knew he had changed what he was going to say – there was something in his expression that gave it away. There had been censure in the way he said her name, now when he spoke there was nothing but a reasonable tone. 'Of course it was not, Alva. However, things did not go as planned.'

'Oh really?' She wanted to stop this, to put an end to her bad behaviour, yet she was out of control. She could remember nothing about this man, yet somehow he stirred something up inside her that was not unpleasant, in fact just then the feeling inside her made her feel breathless, as if she was excited. Something was tugging at her, at the sensitive area of her lower stomach. There was a throbbing too, deep inside her, that made her twist a little to one side and then to twist back again.

'One of my tenants had an accident, a serious accident; I had to arrange to have him flown to the mainland.'

'Oh.' Her lips pursed a little. 'What happened?'

'He was doing some repairs to the roof of his barn, I am afraid he fell and he has fractures in both legs. Thank God he did not damage either his spine or his head.'

'Yes, that is – well, sort of lucky.'

His lips moved in a small smile. 'Fortunate more than lucky,' he said.

'Sorry,' she murmured.

'I have some coffee, would you like some before we ride back?'

'Yes, please.'

He went into his saddle-bag and produced a flask and two tiny cups. 'Shall we sit a moment?'

'Yes.'

Alva sat a little away from the horses. The sun was glorious now – it was so still and peaceful and perfect. His horse nuzzled her horse's neck affectionately; she thought it lovely and said so.

'If horses feel emotion, then you could say that he has always had feelings for her.'

He poured their coffee; it was thick and dark and hot, deliciously so.

'This is good. I'm sorry.'

'Why are you sorry that it is good coffee?'

She mumbled a little laugh. 'No, I mean about running off.'

'You seem to have a habit of doing that, Alva. It is nothing new.'

'Did I do that before?'

'Yes, you did.'

'Why?'

'We would have a disagreement and you would go off. Other times you would just. . . .' He shrugged.

'What?'

'Just disappear for hours, I could never find you.'

'Pretty childish, eh? Playing hide and seek, or maybe not. Perhaps I just needed space. I imagine all this,' she moved her arm expressively, 'was so new to me. Or was it just stupid childlike behaviour?'

'Not necessarily that. I think you needed time on your own to reflect.'

'And of course living in a two up and two down, I had to leave the house.' She could not resist the statement. He understood and he smiled.

'Perhaps you thought that you had no stake in the palazzo.'

'Well I didn't really, did I?'

'It was your home as well as mine,' he stated firmly. 'But you had issues with that.'

'It's hardly surprising. I mean from all accounts I am just an ordinary girl.'

Now he chuckled. 'Am I an extraordinary man?'

She wanted to say, of course you are, how could you not be? You are the most handsome man I am sure I have ever seen, you are rich, you are titled and you ooze Italian sex appeal. But she couldn't say that to him. Instead she said. 'I imagine I thought you different. I mean, an Italian aristocrat is hardly Bill Brown from Battersea.'

'Who is he?' he asked. 'An old boyfriend?'

She laughed. 'No, I mean just an ordinary man.'

'I am an ordinary male. As you found, I think.'

'What do you mean?'

He sighed and stared ahead, looking at the blue ocean and pondering on how to answer.

'That if you cut me I bleed.'

She gasped. She had not expected that. 'I hurt you, is that it?'

'You hurt my pride, Alva. That is different from hurting me.'

'What did I do?'

'Alva, I don't want to do this. Suffice to say we had our problems. When you regain your memory you will know what you did and why. If I were to tell you, you would only have my side of it and that would be unfair.'

She grabbed a handful of silvery sand and let it trickle through her fingers. The grains were her past; it had spilled away from her, would she ever get it back? Did she even want it back?

She bowed her head, sighing softly. This blank page was terrible. The churning feelings inside her were terrible – the whole was such a mess.

His arm came around her, it was the first time he had touched her. She felt the skin at his wrist touching her neck, and it gave her a fizz of delight like a little electric shock.

'I think we should go now, Alva. I am sorry, I should have spoken to you before, but it has been painful for me too. That is a selfish statement, but I can't help it.'

Alva glanced at him and then nodded her agreement, he moved his hand from her skin and she felt very cold and very alone. Daring herself to look at him Alva was not surprised to see that she could not read his expression, yet felt that same kind of melting feeling that would be her undoing if she let it.

'Do you need help?' he asked.

'For what?' she dared herself to be reckless and funny.

'To mount your horse.'

'Me? Of course I don't.' And as if to prove a point she went to her horse, took the bridle and in one smooth jump after putting her foot in the stirrup, mounted the animal. 'There,' she announced and in case he had been doubtful added. 'How about that?'

'Perfect,' he said, and went to do the same.

They rode in silence back the way she had come; he was a little in front of her. It seemed that the stallion might be fond of Star but he wanted to show the mare who was boss, rather like his owner, she thought.

They left the horses with the groom and Luca suggested they go and shower and meet in half an hour.

'We can talk at lunch,' he said, 'or before we eat if you prefer.'

'I'd prefer that,' she said, 'before lunch I mean.'

'I'll see you in the sun lounge.'

He left her standing in the hall, not running up the stairs at her side but going through one of the doors off the lounge. Shrugging, she ran up the stairs and when she got to her room pulled off the shirt and trousers, leaving a thin layer of sand on the tiles in the bathroom. Her wet underwear she put in the sink, put in the plug and filled the bowl with warm water.

Catching a glance of herself in the mirror above the sink, she saw that her eyes looked larger and her cheeks flushed. There was something different about her; perhaps it was the exercise and the fresh air. She determined to do more. She had to get well and fit and then escape this place. There was something about it . . . she shivered, trying to wonder where that had come from. Of course she had lost her child here and then her marriage, but there was something more, there had to be! In frustration, Alva rubbed her temples as if this would release what was buried but there was nothing but an intuitive thought that there was more to everything than she was seeing. People were tiptoeing around her, masking the truth.

After her shower, she went to the wardrobe and took out fresh underwear and a pale green silk dress. It skimmed her body, fitting at the waist but with its boat-shaped neckline looking fetching but definitely not sexy. Eschewing make-up, she left her bedroom and went downstairs. Luca was already there, he had a drink, something pale and light. He asked if she would like some – it was wine, from his own vineyard. She rarely took wine at lunch as it made her sleepy but because of her state of mind she decided to make an exception.

'Alva,' he said her name softly, almost like a sigh. 'I get no pleasure out of telling you this.'

'What do you mean?'

'It isn't pleasant and I don't want to hurt you.'

'I can take it. I have to take it. I don't want to live in a void, not knowing what happened to my baby.'

'Sit down.' It was a command. She thought for a moment to

disobey him but realized that this was the wrong time for such one-upmanship. It was important she let him talk and not get him so angry that he changed his mind.

Sitting on the two-seater sofa, she nervously composed herself, holding her knees tightly together. He did not sit next to her, but chose one of the armchairs, after dragging it close to the sofa.

'You were very ill, I mean really sick. You could not eat without vomiting and that went on for a long time. You had all the bad things and none of the good. We went to a specialist but there was nothing they could do for you. When you got over the sickness, you grew quite quickly, for someone so slender. . . .' He shrugged. 'You said you felt like a beached whale and I am sure that is how it was. Of course you were depressed – no one could blame you, Alva, least of all me. I felt so inadequate, which for me is a rare feeling. I think you were more depressed than I realized. It went deeper than surface depression. When you lost the baby. . . .' He paused, looking deeply into her eyes. Her heart swelled in her breast, there was an ominous thud and then there was a rush of pain, almost as if she could remember how it felt. Luca looked so tortured and surprising her, she felt pain because of that too. She did not want him to experience this pain again and yet she needed to know, had to know everything.

'Was that why we split up? I mean because I was depressed when I lost the baby?'

He studied her, seeming to peel away all the layers she had built up to protect herself from revealing her feelings. She wanted to crawl at the black veil that was keeping things from her. Luca did not want to go on, she saw that and she wondered why that could be. She knew she had fallen down the stairs, which had caused her baby to die moments after his birth.

Alfredo had told her that she had gone through a long and

terrible labour, that he had wanted her to have a caesarean section but she had not wanted it, fearing that might make it more dangerous for her baby. He lived for a moment, Alfredo had told her and she had seen his tiny little body but then he was gone and nothing they did could revive him.

'How did you feel?' She asked Luca. 'When you heard that your son died, brought into life too soon because I was stupid enough to fall down the stairs!'

She saw his complexion pale, his lips thin. 'I was there, Alva. I was there all the time. You see, then I didn't know how bad it had been. I only found that out a day later.'

'Found out what?' she demanded. 'Luca, you have to tell me everything. It's so unfair that I'm living my life in this blackness. I need to know *everything*; surely you have to understand that?'

'Alva,' he murmured. 'You should really wait until you are stronger.'

'Well, that's going to do me good, knowing there is something that I am too weak to understand! You have to tell me now, Luca, please, don't make me beg.'

'Beg. Do you think I want that? I just wanted you to have a safe haven until you regained your memory. That's all. I did not want to drag you through it all again.'

'Luca,' she warned. 'Please do not prevaricate.'

'I'm sorry – I'm sorry I have to say it now and I am sorry that I am going to make you suffer. Believe me, Alva I don't want to do this. You did not fall down the stairs, Alva, you threw yourself down.'

He did not believe her and she was making herself even angrier by demanding that he did. No, she cried, no definitely no! She could not do something like that. Not only was it a despicable thing to do, she would be too afraid to do such a thing. Only yesterday she had been terrified by what could have happened when she had fallen down the stairs. She would *never* have done it deliberately.

'Why won't you believe me?'

'Because you were not alone, Alva, someone saw you do it.'

'No! Who was it?'

He stared at her, his eyes revealing nothing of his feelings. 'Was it Renata? Renata and you believed her, even though you knew she hated me.'

'Hated you? She might have disliked you but she was a girl and hate is too strong a word.'

'Oh yes, it would be. You always took her side against me, I can see it all now; that's why I was depressed and unhappy, it had nothing to be with how I felt physically.'

'Alva, you can remember nothing so you can't know that. And,' he paused, 'it was not Renata.'

That came as a blow for she could not imagine anyone else who would want to lie. Not any of the servants. She had been at the palazzo only days but she knew the servants liked her. There was no one on the staff who had an interest in telling lies about her, unless— 'Who was it?'

'Antonio.'

'Antonio? But you said he was my friend, or you implied as much.'

'He was someone you used to talk to, quite a lot actually but I would hardly call him your friend.'

'And he said he saw me throw myself down the stairs, *deliberately*?'

'He tried to catch you.'

'I'm sure he did,' she murmured. How could she know she did not do that? She tried to scale the blank walls in her mind. It was instinct that guided her and instinct she believed more than her husband. Oh, maybe he had been told what she had done – but that did not make it the truth. There was nothing in her that told her she could do that – cowardice? No far more than that, a sense of morality. She could not have killed her own child, no matter how depressed or unhappy she was. *She could not.*

'The baby was a boy. I called him Alessandro, for my father, and he is buried here. Close to the summerhouse.'

She felt it inside herself now, the rush of feeling, the reason she had been lured to the spot. Some foggy memory, some need to be there.

'What did I do?'

'You never came home again. You left.'

'From?'

'You were in the hospital on the mainland. You stayed there about three months.'

'Oh yes? Incarcerated, was I?'

'That is rather dramatic, Alva.'

'Was I being treated for a mental condition or not?'

He sighed. 'You were treated for depression.'

'How fortunate I was not imprisoned.'

'Why would you be imprisoned?'

'I murdered my son.'

'Alva. . . .'

'That's what you believe, that's what I'm accused of!'

'Alva, you wanted to harm yourself as well.'

'Oh sure I did. I'm sorry, Luca, you should never have asked me here. I don't think I want to stay with someone who supposedly loved me then can coolly accuse me of doing such a thing.'

'Alva, you were not yourself.'

'No, I wasn't. Excuse me, I don't want any lunch.'

He did not protest but let her walk out of the room. She did not go to her bedroom but out into the grounds, running now towards the summerhouse. The little grave was to the side of the summerhouse, in a plot of gaily coloured tiny flowers, a small headstone a name, Alessandro. She translated the other words easily enough. At least he had included her, if only by her title Contessa Mazareeze.

Falling to her knees, she ran a finger around the carved name. She was six months pregnant; the baby was old enough perhaps to have lived had he been born as a premature baby, instead of one who had been damaged by her supposed action. Had it hurt him, her body bouncing down those marble stairs? Please let him not have felt pain, she pleaded, her tears now watering the tiny flowers.

I am so sorry, Alessandro, something terrible happened to you but I know it was not because I wanted it to. One day I will remember, I have to remember and then, well then we shall see.

She lay, curled up on the small plot, unconscious of time until Luca came to find her. She let him help her to her feet, one of her feet had cramp and she had to stamp her foot to bring the blood tingling back.

'You have to eat a little,' he murmured. 'It is turning chilly, you are cold.'

'I'm OK, I can manage now,' she shrugged out of his arm.

They walked back to the house side by side, the clock in the hall told her it was turned two, so she must to have been with Alessandro for two hours.

She took a little cream of chicken soup and a slice of bread but refused the pasta. It took all her time to swallow the soup but she knew she had to keep up her strength. There were things that needed to be done.

When she had finished, she finally looked at Luca. He had eaten little and was staring absently into space. 'When I asked if you loved me, you said the sex was good. I thought you meant to hurt me, Luca, only now I see you were telling the truth. You couldn't have loved me otherwise you would have known that I would never have done such a thing.'

'Alva. . . .'

She held up her hand for his silence. 'Let me finish, then I won't bring it up again. I must have been a real pain, droning on about how I felt; I can imagine how irritating that must have been. You were probably so happy that I was pregnant, you were happy about it weren't you?'

He nodded.

'Italians love children, I know that. Not from what I remember but something that I instinctively know. We should have enjoyed it all together, but my body, I suppose, wouldn't let me enjoy it. Well, it happens. But I know, Luca, that no matter what I was going through, I would never have done that. I couldn't have done it. I don't know why this man lied to you but lie he did. I don't blame you; if you had really loved me you would have believed *me*.'

She folded her hands in her lap, withdrawing them from his view because they trembled. Her voice was coming out loud and clear but inside she was a trembling mass of insecurity, yet she could not show him that. She had to be strong and not crumble. If only he realized how much she longed for him to hold her, to tell her that he believed her, that he would do anything in his power to discover the truth, but he would not do that. The people that he had around him were trusted. His daughter, this man Antonio, it was she, his young wife, who had been the cuckoo in the nest.

'I don't imagine I am Miss Perfect. I don't know what I am really but I know I am not a baby killer, Luca. . . .'

'No one would suggest you were,' Luca was haughty once more, his expression stern, his feelings, if he had any, hidden away just as were hers. 'You were depressed, Alva, very depressed; you did not wish to kill the baby, you wished to kill yourself.'

She almost smiled, but it was not really an attempt at a smile, her lips had a bitter twist. 'Sounds like a good story. You know what, Luca? In the hospital in London, after the accident, I could have died, I was on the very brink of death, but I fought back. They said I was such a fighter, I amazed them all by how much I wanted to survive. That doesn't sound to me like someone who would commit suicide and – let's not mince words, be a baby murderer too. No matter how depressed I was I would still have that will to survive. And if I hadn't, well don't you think I would have made a better job of it. I mean Luca, throwing myself down the stairs – how dramatic is that and how dangerous? I could have ended up in a wheel chair for the rest of my life – paralysed, brain dead, *whatever*!' She stood, pushing her chair back against the table, grasping the carved top to give her strength. 'No, Luca that is not my way of doing things. I'm sorry you thought so little of me that you could think that, but there you go,' it was her turn to shrug. 'Without love there is nothing.'

'I did love you,' he said quietly, 'I said it was all sex to hurt you, just as you thought. I was crazy about you, Alva.'

'But not enough, Luca. Not when it came to taking my word for something. But you know what, I'm going to find out the truth, Luca – somehow, some way and then, then I can go away, and then I will find some peace.'

CHAPTER THREE

THEY ate dinner together and managed to make polite conversation on several evenings. Alva was interested in learning from Luca what she had done with her life. Luca explained that she helped him by visiting the sick, helping people with problems when they preferred to speak to the contessa rather than the conte. She was also his hostess when he entertained and when he had to travel, she accompanied him. Her life had been quite full.

'If I can help in anyway while I am here, then please let me,' she said. He told her there would be a dinner party in three weeks. Some very important guests would attend and if she would be his hostess he would be pleased. Of course she agreed, only by going out and meeting people might there be a chance of regaining at least some of her memory. Skulking indoors would do her no good at all.

She arranged to go to the mainland; she would need the launch and asked Luca to arrange it for her.

Guido waited with her in the car at the port and eventually the launch came into view. 'Here is Antonio,' Guido advised her.

She hid her smile. It was the perfect arrangement – it was what she had hoped for; she could measure the man who had lied about her, and she was curious, too, as to what he could benefit by doing such a thing. Supposedly, they had been friends. Was it even more than friendship? Had she cheated on Luca with one of his employees. She felt it would be improbable but was it impossible?

His appearance surprised her; he was her height and very slim. His hair was fair and his eyes were blue. His features were very attractive and, like the way he dressed, neat. Small nose, thin but perfectly shaped lips. There was something about him that was a little feminine. Instinctively, she knew she had not found herself attracted to him. He was not her type at all. She knew that as surely as she knew her eyes were green. Being fair herself, she always found herself attracted to dark men. When Antonio was compared with Luca, well there was no competition. No, whatever anyone said, she would not have been with this man in any capacity other than perhaps friendship. If she had been lonely, then she would have been glad to have someone to talk to.

Antonio greeted her politely, even taking her hand as he helped her board the launch. Although driving the launch his clothing was very neat. His chinos were well pressed, a white cotton polo shirt was enlivened by a cherry red sweater which was draped over his shoulders, the sleeves fastened across his chest. He wore aviator sunglasses on top of his head. Almost she thought him a caricature for a holiday brochure or a coffee advertisement.

'*Grazie*, Antonio,' she murmured as she boarded, going to sit on the seat closest to the wheel.

'I hope you are feeling better, Contessa?' he asked politely. He did have an easy-on-the ear voice, musical and rich.

'Yes, I'm fine now,' she murmured.

He turned, his complexion paled somewhat, there was a question in his eye. He is wondering if I have remembered things, she thought, and decided not to enlighten him.

'You are completely well?' he asked smoothly, turning the

boat in a wide arc.

'Almost there – in fact, being here has made me recall all kinds of things.'

He gave her a studied look. 'But the conte said you could not remember anything.'

Had Luca really discussed her with this man? The haughty conte telling his woes to one of his employees? It seemed highly unlikely. Alva guessed that Antonio was speculating and that he really knew nothing at all.

'It's a daily thing,' she murmured, 'it is rather as though I am reading a long novel, each day a page is opened in mind. I can't read very fast but there is always a paragraph or two that I can manage.' Stupid metaphor she thought to herself, but it was enough to cause Antonio's body to tense and for his hand to tighten on the wheel.

Eventually he said sternly. 'The conte said I should stay with you in town, Contessa. He was not sure that you would cope well on your own.'

'Antonio, you know how the conte worries. I am perfectly all right, I do assure you. And I intend to do a lot of shopping. That would surely bore you.'

'Not at all, I like shopping.'

'Really, how unusual for a man.'

'Not for an Italian, Contessa!'

'Yes, I forgot. But really I shall be perfectly all right. I shall be happier on my own. I am only going to Primo and maybe a couple of designer shops.'

'Still. . . .' He was going to insist.

'If you are doubtful I will telephone my husband. I have my mobile.' She slid a hand into her commodious tan leather handbag.

'Oh, that is not necessary, Contessa, I do take your word for it.'

So, perhaps Luca had not said any such thing and that

intrigued her. Why should he not wish her to be alone? However, she said no more, and stared out at the far shore as the town grew closer. It troubled her that Luca had implied that she spent a lot of time with this man. Alva felt it hardly credible – there was nothing about him that attracted her. Even had she been lonely he was hardly a wonderful conversationalist. Since their last words he had not spoken to her at all, and had they been friends at one time, there would have had to have been things that he knew she liked to talk about. Something was not right and it was so frustrating to know that the truth of the matter was locked behind the high walls of memory loss.

The town, she found, was a delight. When she left the launch she turned, thinking she would have to concentrate to convince Antonio that she knew where she was going, yet incredibly her feet did seem to remember the way to go.

Turning right, she crossed the cobbled road, took the first street, which was narrow and cobbled, climbed three wide steps and took an immediate left, passing between two tall yellow-painted buildings, and there was the main square open before her. Right across the square was a large sign denoting 'Primo'. Around the square were other fashionable shops, selling leather goods and luxury foods as well as two which displayed very upmarket clothing. It was Claudia who had told her the name of the department store. 'You like it there, Contessa, and will go for coffee and lovely little cakes.' So it had been easy to remember the name of her favourite store when she had been talking to Antonio.

The square was pedestrianized; the sun was out and already people were sitting at the pavement cafés. She did not linger here but went across to Primo and swung through the swing doors with a confidence she did not really feel. Just inside the door was a display of chocolate and a very attractive girl was giving out samples. Alva took one, popping it into her mouth and marvelling at the exquisite taste.

*

Her browsing done, she knew she had just over two hours to kill before she was to meet Antonio and go back. She chose one of the pavement cafés for lunch and at once a table was found for her. The sun was wonderfully warm but not intense, and although the brightly patterned umbrella shaded her head, she could feel the heat on her bare legs. The mobile phone in her bag rang out its gay little tune just as she ordered a slice of pizza and a salad.

It was Luca. His voice caused her heart to leap, melting warmth invaded her. There was something so wonderful about the way he used words. He had a caressing tone, which was even more devastating over the telephone. That was the thing she remembered about him, his voice. He had said the same thing about her. Their very first communication had been over the telephone and it was over the telephone that the spark had first ignited.

In the moments that she spoke to him it did not occur to her that she had remembered something important. She was too intent on what he was saying.

'Buy something stunning,' he murmured. 'To wear at the dinner party. You like Paola's. Where are you?'

'The café Rosa,' she murmured.

'Then it is across the square and to the right. I will call her and tell her to expect you, what time would you like to go?'

'Well I don't know, Luca, surely I have dresses.'

'They might not fit. It is very important that you dress well, Alva. Let me call Paola, what time?'

'Well, if you insist.' She checked the slim gold watch at her wrist. 'Will she be there at two?'

'If you are going to be there, she will be.'

'OK, that will give her time to have lunch.'

'She is a wraith. I think she never eats. I will see you later.'

'Yes, and thank you, Luca.'

'*Prego*.' And then he was gone.

After she had eaten she crossed the square leisurely. She took the right as instructed and sure enough there was a shop. There was one dress in the window. The whole shop front screamed 'expensive'. The gold lettering on the window announcing the name Paola was beautifully done. She stood for a moment or two seeking the confidence to go inside and then it came to her. What she had remembered. Turning from the shop she went back into the square, there was a bench and she went to sit on it, oblivious to the passers-by.

Go back, she counselled herself, to the first time that you heard Luca speak. On the telephone, she remembered that. He was calling to speak to her boss but he was not there. Luca asked to leave a message – he did not call himself Count Mazareeze, he just called himself Luca Mazareeze. He said in a warm and friendly way, 'Do you wish me to spell it for you?' And she had laughed and spelt it out for him. '*Parla Italiano, signorina*?'

'A little,' she murmured. She spoke more than a little but felt shy about using the language to this man with the intriguing voice.

Alva sat for sometime on the bench, just staring at the square without seeing anything. She remembered everything that they had said and how she had felt, that lovely gushing feeling that was overwhelming, the flutter of her heart, the breathlessness. But that was all; she could remember nothing on either side of that conversation. Yet it was something, it was momentous to her!

The clock struck the half hour, Paola was waiting for her, she could not spare any more time to sit and dream. Standing, she made her way back to the shop, and when she arrived she went straight in, pushing open the door with more confidence than she actually felt.

Paola was thin – she saw that Luca had not exaggerated – and she was older than Alva had imagined her to be. Her black hair was obviously dyed and there was a pinched look about her eyes, yet when she smiled the woman exuded warmth and enthusiasm.

'My favourite client,' she murmured, 'has returned. Welcome, Contessa.'

It occurred to Alva that the woman probably said the same thing to every one of her customers yet she did not care. The warmth the woman exuded boosted her self-esteem and she willingly gave herself over to her.

There was only one dress really and they both agreed on it. Others were tried but Alva and Paola came back to the first one. Midnight blue – a bustier top, falling away to a full skirt. The dark colour was set off by her creamy skin, the bustier emphasized the smallness of her waist and the skirt swirled elegantly around her hips. 'Midnight blue is your colour. Of course blondes look wonderful in black but this is so flattering for you, Contessa.'

Buoyed up by the woman's obvious honesty, she purchased the dress, and then checked her watch before making her way to where the launch had dropped her.

The sun was sinking over the horizon in a bright orange ball. The burning streaks across the sky were reflected on the blue sea, making it look as if it was on fire. Alva paused for a moment to drink in the view. Across the bay, the island could be seen rising out of the water in a blaze of golden light; it was a spectacular sight.

She saw the boat; someone was standing on the quay alongside it. Someone taller than Antonio. She crossed the road to the quayside and only as she drew near did she realize it was not a stranger. The man standing by the boat was her husband, Count Mazareeze himself.

He had to have heard her heels striking the pavement, for

he turned. He smiled a greeting. Even in the wine-coloured cashmere shirt, he looked elegant, cream chinos had never looked as good as they did on him. He did not need the posing accessory of a sweater tied around him, or aviator sunglasses on his head, he just looked good in anything. He possessed an effortless elegance that, she knew, would always steal her breath.

'This is a surprise.'

'I had something else for Antonio to do; besides I had someone to see in town. Come aboard.'

He held out his hand and she took it, stepping on to the deck with as much elegance as she could muster. He took her bag from her. Like Paola's windows, the bag was stylish, black and shiny, tiny gold name in the top corner. There was nothing garish about Paola's marketing.

'I won't peek.'

'You'd better not. You have to trust both our judgements.'

'I do,' he smiled down at her. It seemed a long time since she had seen him smile like that. It had not been while she had been in Italy; remarkably she knew she remembered it from before. There were little breaks of light in the darkness but she said nothing to him about them. It was too soon and she did not want either of them to feel optimistic. There had to be brighter chinks of light before she shared them with him.

He went to the wheel and started the boat's engine. She did not follow him but sat just outside the cabin admiring the play of scarlet ribbons across the turquoise water. Halfway across the stretch of water, she turned back and looked at the town. The sun was casting red streaks of light over the honey-coloured buildings, dancing across the terracotta roofs.

'This is so beautiful,' she called to Luca. He turned and looked at her.

'Yes, it is, very beautiful.'

Something in the way he said it made her catch her breath. Did he really mean the town? He could not have been referring to *her*, yet if he was not why had he looked at her in that way. In what way? Her mind teased. As if he liked what he saw, a little voice echoed through her, very much. Nonsense, he does not care for me, he cannot forgive me for what he thinks I did. He is being nice because he wants something from me. And will you give him what he wants? The teasing question made her limbs melt; she felt the throb of desire deep inside her, parts of her body puckered as if for his kiss. What he wants, girl, her sensible side spoke up, is for you to be the perfect hostess for his dinner party. That is what he wants and *nothing* else.

On the morning of the party the palazzo buzzed with the sound of preparations. Delivery vans would come and go in rapid succession. Flowers were brought; Claudia had the girls polishing the silver, and then set the table, calling for Alva to inspect it when it was done.

She had ordered pink and cream roses as the centre piece, it was perfect, nicer even than she had expected. The napery was cream damask, the tableware the finest Limoges. Everything glistened and shone and looked elegant but welcoming. Tall silver candelabra housed long slender cream candles which, when lighted, would reflect on the fine crystal glassware. 'It's perfect,' she said to Guido who was acting as butler. He had polished the huge chandelier and had raised it again and it shone in the patches of sunlight that spilled into the room, in a rainbow of light. Since she had been here they had never used the formal dining-room and she had not realized what a truly magnificent room it was.

She had just applied her make-up when a tap on the bedroom door disturbed her. Alva knew it would be her husband on the other side. Only the maids came to her room and they always just came in. Pulling the towelling robe more closely to her, she called, 'Come in'. She was not disappointed but she was shattered to see him again. In black tie he was even more magnificent. Of course she knew immediately that she had seen him like that before. She could visualize it, the very first time she had seen him, a large room with a high ceiling, lots of people, clinking glasses and then there was Luca, and straight away she had known that he was the Conte Mazareeze.

'Are you all right?' he asked, his voice kind.

'I'm fine,' Deciding to be honest. 'I'm a little nervous.'

'That's natural but I do know you will be wonderful. You did not show me your dress but I thought that these would not come amiss – they would hardly clash with anything.'

He handed her a red velvet box. With nervous fingers she opened it. Diamonds sparkled up at her – these were no rhinestones, she knew that right off, there was too much fire coming off them. They were small and exquisitely set; a necklace and drop ear-rings. 'They're beautiful.'

'They are a family treasure, permit me, Alva.'

She handed him the box and turned her back, lifting her hair off her neck. The diamonds were cold against her overheated flesh. 'You smell good,' she murmured, catching a whiff of cologne.

'So do you,' he murmured.

'I haven't perfumed up yet,' she laughed nervously. His fingers, brushing against her flesh as he fastened the clasp, caused a pleasurable fluttering at her heart.

'You don't need to; your skin exudes . . . something. . . .'

'Moisturizer,' she murmured.

'I wasn't meaning that.'

'I know but . . . just don't, Luca.'

'Don't what?'

'Tease me.'

He was silent, his hand moved from her neck and she heard him step back from her.

'Of course, and you are quite right. I apologize, Alva.'

'So you should!' Alva could not stop the reprimand.

'Alva, it is difficult to forget how once we were. But I know it would be taking advantage of you because you cannot remember – remember how it was!'

'You think I can't decide what I want because I can't remember, Luca? You have a lot to learn about women if you do think that.'

'A man always has much to learn about women. It was a man that said that women were made to be loved and not understood.'

'Isn't that contradictory?'

'I am sorry?'

'In your case.'

'Oh, I see. Probably it is, but I was speaking generally.'

'Well,' she turned. 'Perhaps I would like you to take advantage of me, Luca.'

She heard him gasp, or was it a groan.

'This is not the time,' he said at last, checking his watch. 'Certainly not for this kind of conversation. I'll see you downstairs, in the sitting-room, Alva. Our guests should be arriving any time now.'

'I'll be there. I don't intend to make a grand entrance, you know. I have only to slip into my dress.'

He went to leave, only pausing at the door. 'You don't need to make a grand entrance, Alva. You will be sensational just being in the room.' Then he was gone.

She undid her robe and found herself smiling. She had disturbed him; it was something that she liked to do and would most certainly do again.

*

Luca's guests did not faze her. On the contrary, she felt quite at ease. At that brief moment when the first arrivals were brought into the sitting-room, Alva felt her heart lurch with a combination of fear and apprehension. They came across to her, a tall woman with brown hair and eyes, attractive more than beautiful, and the man, smaller than she, but with something of Luca in his features.

The woman – Luca's sister in law – allowed her lips to form a smile, but her eyes did not light up and instead, they tore across Alva's face, and then down over her gown, lingering on – her body tensing – the diamonds at Alva's neck. Alva felt the dislike emanating from Sophia Mazareeze but she found herself able to ignore it. Her husband, Paolo, also had little warmth but he hid it better than the woman. It was their slight antipathy towards her that gave Alva a spurt of courage. It doesn't matter, she thought, they are nothing to me. They never were. I've done this kind of thing before. In the job I had there were a lot of backstabbers and envious people, I didn't let them get me down and got on with my job. At school I faced up to some bullying too. These thoughts flashed in and out of her mind like a flickering reel of film but she felt them lodge in her mind. She could examine them later; they were not going to fade away.

Curtis Trevor and his wife Maryanne were delightful. They had that open friendliness of Americans and at once their attitude to her gave her even more confidence. They knew nothing, they saw only the contessa. They had no previous experience of her and she could be herself and need not worry about what they were thinking. Some of the other people had known her before, apparently, but only slightly. Curtis, a film producer, was hoping to persuade Luca to allow him to film on the island.

Looking across at Luca, as it had passed the time they should be sitting down for dinner, she saw him anxiously looking at his watch. Obviously, there was another guest. Whoever they were, it was extremely rude to be late and not to call.

Excusing herself from Curtis and Maryanne she crossed the room to where Luca was standing. He was in conversation with his brother.

'Excuse me, Luca but what is happening?'

It was Paolo who answered. 'We are waiting for someone, isn't that obvious.'

'Paolo!' Luca hissed between his teeth. Paolo turned his back and went to where his wife was standing.

'I must apologize for his rudeness, it seems.'

'Not at all, he can apologize himself, but I doubt he will. We are waiting for someone then?'

'Yes, it is—'

But there was a flutter and a little cry of delight from Sophia Mazareeze. 'Rosa!'

In the doorway stood a small, slender woman. She was dark and alluring. Her gold and green dress draped her perfect little body, enhancing the gentle curves. Her hair was swept showing her face off perfectly. Feature perfect, the woman seemed well aware of the impact her entrance was having and stood still to prolong the moment. Her dark eyes scanned the room, alighted on Luca and her full red lips parted in a smile. 'Luca,' she exclaimed. 'Forgive me. . . .' She came towards them, her hands outstretched. Luca accepted her hands and bending kissed her cheek.

'My car would not start; I was in such a panic.'

Alva watched the performance and indeed that was what it was and did not believe it for a moment. Had her car really refused to start she would have called. What she had wanted was to create impact and she had succeeded.

'Rosa, you remember Alva?' He stood to one side, giving Alva full stage.

'Oh yes, of course, but Alva will not remember me,' she

flicked a look at Alva, and then returned her gaze to Luca. Possessively, she slid an arm through his arm. Turning back to Alva she murmured. 'Luca and I are very old friends.'

'Are you?' Alva murmured back. 'That must be nice for both of you. Would you care for a drink, Rosa, or will you be ready to eat?'

'I do not drink, Alva.' She squeezed Luca's arm. 'I have very few vices.'

Just one or two, Alva thought, flirting, posing and being completely in love with yourself. But she showed no animosity. Anyway how could she? Luca did not belong to her. Their marriage was over. He could do as he liked and with whom. Oh, my, but did it have to hurt so much?

Rosa d'Casta dominated the dinner table; she flirted outrageously with the men and ignored the women, apart from Sophia who anyway seemed to hang on to her every word. What an obnoxious woman, Alva thought. Obviously, whatever she was in my past, a friend she was not.

Curtis Trevor though remained unimpressed; he and his wife spent the time talking to Alva. He said, flirting with her, 'You ought to be in pictures, you know. The camera would love you.'

'I bet you say that to all the girls.'

'He'd better not,' Maryanne laughed.

'No, honey, have no fear. What did you do before becoming the contessa, Alva, were you an actress?'

'Heavens, no. I believe I worked for a politician.'

'You believe?' Maryanne asked puzzled.

'I really think I should explain,' Alva said. 'I was in an accident. A hit and run. I lost my memory; I only know what Luca has told me.'

It was good to be able to explain to someone sympathetic and the couple were kind and very supportive. When she had finished Curtis asked who Rosa was.

'I have no idea, a friend of the family I think.'

'Gee, she's some—'

'Curtis,' Maryanne cautioned.

'Yeah, sorry. So how do you cope, it must be so strange?'

'Well, I need to try to get better,' she glanced down the table. Rosa was now in deep conversation with Luca, pouting and widening her eyes. 'For Luca's sake, if not my own.'

It seemed very old-fashioned to Alva, but after dinner Luca took the men off to the library. Of course she knew the reason, he wanted to talk business, but she found she was a little uncomfortable with some of the women. As if sensing her unease Maryanne came and took her arm. 'I would love to see the garden, will it be too dark?'

'The garden adjacent to the house? We have light; of course we can go. . . .'

She made no excuse and drifted away through the glass doors. They walked along the covered terrace, arm in arm, and down through the rose garden. It was a warm evening, warmer than it had been the whole time she had been in Santa Catarina. It was hard to believe it was late October.

For Alva, just having a normal conversation about gardens and plants and Italy in general was a pleasure. Feeling relaxed for the first time that evening, Alva forgot all about the spiteful Rosa and her unfriendly in-laws.

Luca came to find them to announce that their guests were leaving. He seemed cold and distant and his attitude drove the pleasant feelings out of her.

After the guests had left, leaving behind Sophia, Paolo and Rosa, Alva apologized but said she was feeling very tired and would need to go to bed.

'We won't disturb you,' Rosa said, barely hiding her pleasure at the news that Alva was leaving the party.

'I am quite sure that nothing will disturb me, Rosa. Goodnight.'

She was seething, the anger boiling away inside her. If she had been herself, then Alva knew, with certainty, that she would have been well able to put out Rosa's fire. Instinct told her that the old Alva was no pushover. If she had held down a good job in the world of politics it was obvious she was no shrinking violet. If she could survive that kind of backstabbing atmosphere, then she could certainly hold her own with a spiteful, pampered person like Rosa. However, she was not herself. She hadn't the energy to fight and was not even certain that she wanted to, or even if she had the right to. Luca was not hers and nor was this palazzo anything to do with her any more. She was as much a guest in its luxurious walls as was Rosa.

Once in her room, she peeled off her beautiful gown and carefully hung it in the wardrobe. Slipping out of her silk lingerie, she changed into a scarlet satin robe. As she sat at her dressing-table brushing her hair, she realized the diamonds were still about her neck. Putting down the brush and raising her hands, she unclipped the clasp. Carefully, she laid the sparkling gems on the dressing-table top. They were beautiful. In the soft light of the dressing-table lamp they gave off a whole kaleidoscope of colour.

The door creaked open and, turning she was surprised to see it was Luca. He had not knocked. Still angry about Rosa d'Casta, she reminded him that he had omitted to knock.

'Why should I knock, you are my wife. I don't have to knock on doors to see my wife.'.

'I am your soon-to-be ex-wife, Luca.'

'But you are not yet. What are you doing?'

'Getting ready for bed I—'

'I don't mean that!' he snapped. 'I mean by disappearing and leaving guests to fend for themselves? Going to bed as soon as the Americans left.'

'The Americans left with some Italians, Luca. I can hardly

be branded a racist for that! Besides, you had your surrogate hostess, you did not need me.'

'What do you mean, my surrogate hostess? Do you mean Rosa?'

'You know very well who I mean. God, I can smell her on you from here!'

He came across to her, walking quite serenely. He is not even going to bother to deny it, she thought. He reached her side and looked down at the sparkling diamonds. He lifted them from the tabletop and slipped them in his pocket.

'I didn't intend to keep them; there was no need for you to come here for them.'

'I will be putting them back in the safe. Have you any idea how much they are worth?' But he spoke mildly.

'No idea and I could not care less.'

'No, you never did – I used to like that about you.'

'Like what?'

'Your unmaterialistic attitude to life.'

'Oh, something I got right!'

He was standing behind her now she watched his reflection in the mirror – he was staring at her really hard, his mouth a hard line. He is angry with me, she thought.

His hands went on to her shoulders; she watched fascinated as they massaged the heavy satin of her robe; it felt good to have his hands doing that, easing her tension but awakening something far more potent. The manipulating of the material caused it to gape a little; he saw it, saw the shadowy darkness between her breasts. Bending his head he captured her ear in his mouth, his tongue seeking out every little crevice. She leant back against him, her head against his belly. Slowly, his hands slid down her front, parting the material as they went, exposing her breasts, her nipples were hard and at the alert, revealing their eagerness for his touch. He did not disappoint, the hands slid down and cupped each breast, his thumbs moving over the hard peaks.

He drew her up slowly out of the chair, turning her to face him. Her bottom rested against the dressing-table for a microsecond, until his hands went there, beneath the satin robe, to cup the globes of her behind, drawing her into an embrace that left no doubt of how he felt about her just then.

Eagerly her body arched against him though she half did not want to be this way with him, wanted not to be so available, part of her wanted to send him away, yet that other part of her ... the womanly had ... different ideas and more powerful urges.

'I want to smell of you,' he groaned, 'I want to fill myself with your essence. I want you all over me, do you know that, Alva ... do you?'

She moved her head in denial, her lips parting, her tongue flickering over her lips provocatively. 'Alva,' he moaned. 'Alva. ...' He bent his head, taking her lips in his, sliding his tongue deep in her mouth, where her tongue met and played with his. Her hands travelled him, forcing up his shirt, seeking his back, playing her fingers along his spine, moving around his front, down his pants, over the hard firmness of his belly, feeling the luxurious tickle of body hair, that hair that she knew arrowed down his belly, spreading between his thighs.

'Don't do that ... not yet—' He gasped against her hair now, dragging out her hand and holding it tight while he bent her backwards and fitted her pulsating centre against him. She moved against him, unashamedly allowing him to know just what she desired.

With a burst of savage and erotic words, he lifted her off her feet, going with her to the bed and laying her down. He pulled at his own clothes while she lay as he had left her, her robe open, her body arched. She knew – remembered in a wild blinding flash – how it had been. He was a glorious lover, she had found complete ecstasy with him, she longed for it again, made urgent demands, tried to stop herself from tripping over into nothingness until he was where she desired him, deep inside her.

He came then, moving up the bed, mounting her, finding her lips. 'Do I smell of you now, Alva . . . mm? Taste me, taste you on me. . . .'

She moaned her delight, reaching up to kiss his mouth, to plunge her tongue against his. He was there now, his maleness pulsating against her. Her hands slid down his body, holding him, guiding him, and then he was joined with her, they were one, and she could explore with him that other place, that nothingness – that place that was everything and gave her completeness.

They lay still, the early morning sun spilling light into the room, she was replete, satiated, and it had been wonderful. He had not lied about that aspect then, the sex was good but for her it was more than sex. Anyone could have sex but this . . . she sighed, this was different. Inside her was such love, it felt so new it overwhelmed her but it was there, she had merely forgotten how it felt. She thought she had perhaps mislaid it during their trouble, but it had not gone away. Of course she could not speak for him, who knew what he *really* felt. He had not said, *Ti amo*, but, her highly developed conscience reminded her, neither had she. She had to have said everything except those very special words.

They were insatiable, making love as if there would be no more opportunity. Was it instinct that told her what he enjoyed, what it was drove him wild, or was there an inkling in her mind? He adored her body, he liked to gaze at her, was filled with a sensual delight when she mounted him, it drove him wild, he called out to her. '*Sei bella*. . . .' Beautiful, beautiful.

Now his hand stroked her head tenderly, and she lay at peace, her head against his chest, enjoying the steady thud of his heart beating against her cheek.

'I didn't come to do that, you know,' he murmured.

'You didn't?'

'No, I came to be awkward.'

'Oh really, you mean you do awkward?'

He chuckled. '*Prego*, so I can be a beast at times.'

'I wouldn't say that,' she smiled contented. 'Awkward is better. Stubborn and stand-offish. . . .'

'Please, let me leave with some dignity.'

'So why did you not just be awkward?'

'Ah, *bella*. . . .' He kissed her head. 'I have a thing for scarlet satin. You won't remember but I do, I bought you that robe. We both liked it, it feels good, it looks good—'

'And by golly it does me good!'

They burst out laughing and he hugged her to him.

'That is one of our old jokes. You remember?'

'No, but I do remember the line, from an advertisement I think, long ago,' she said.

'Yes, you told me so. Funny how it stayed in your mind when other things did not.'

Her antenna pricked up and waved its spindly arms about, but no, he was not accusing her – merely stating fact.

'Peripheral memory,' she said. 'Learned stuff. I know how to write, to read, and to calculate. Ride a horse, drive a car. . . .' She smiled. 'Make love?'

He bent and kissed her nose. 'Oh yes, you did not forget that.'

'Should we get up?'

'Do you want to?'

'Not really, maybe we should take a bath – have some coffee. What do you have to do today?'

'I just want to be with you, *bella*!'

CHAPTER FOUR

HE had long gone and still she stayed lazily content in bed. The day had been glorious and the night . . . oh the night, she sighed. Who was this man? Not the austere and rather cold conte of her recent recall, but a man of warmth and fun and humour. A man both loving and passionate.

They had dined in her room, sat out on the balcony and talked of inconsequential matters. Now as she lay there her mind flooded with images. She remembered now, as if it was yesterday, how they had met – the first time they had made love but not beyond that. The feelings she had felt came rushing in on her, overwhelming her. It was like falling in love for the very first time and that was what had happened. She had never been in love before, yet the first moment she met the Conte Luca Mazareeze was the time she fell in love.

His voice on the telephone, she had recalled that, so warm and teasing. She made herself not picture how he would look, she knew from experience how that could bring disappointment. How many princes had she imagined from the voice, only on meeting them to find out they were frogs! The conte, though, was even more than she could have imagined. Tall, and elegant and charming. 'Oh, gosh,' she had said to the girl standing at her side.

'Oh gosh and then gosh, gosh, and more – and he is coming

across,' the girl – and Alva could not bring her face to mind – did a little twirl but it was not her he spoke to. He had said. 'You must be Alva,'

'I must?' she had asked, then wanted to kick herself for being stupid.

'Am I wrong?'

'But how do you know?'

He smiled warmly. 'I spoke to your boss, I said you were charming and you had the most delightful voice and he, although I did not ask, told me that you were blonde and pretty and would not be a disappointment in the flesh.'

'Oh really!' She flushed angrily. She was not sure that was quite what she wanted to hear. How dare her boss talk about her like that, as if she were part of some deal or other?

'Don't be angry with him, he was not lying. Should he have said you were old and plain?'

'He shouldn't have said anything. My appearance has nothing to do with my position.'

He laughed into her eyes. 'If you think that you are deceiving yourself.'

'What do you mean?' Her back was well and truly up, just what was he implying?

'Nothing,' he said, 'nothing at all.'

'I'm very good at my job.'

'I don't doubt it, Alva.'

He turned then and walked away. She turned to say something to her companion but she had gone. Alva was standing alone. Turning, she walked away, going to the ladies room. Really, Tony Laker took too much on himself.

Ah, she stirred in bed – that was his name. The man who was her boss, the politician who had done something wrong. Tony Laker. A rather squat, arrogant man. She could see him now. But for all his faults, and he had many, the job had been good. She had liked it, the travelling, and the excitement of being around important people. How shallow she had to have been, she thought, but no, she was young but she was not that impressionable. She had quickly learned that many of those important people had feet of clay. But not the conte. No, never Conte Mazareeze. He was just perfect.

If he had not been so stunning she knew she would have laughed off what he had said.

It angered her because of the way he made her feel, not because of what he had said. She had heard worse many times before.

A knock on the door disturbed her thoughts and to her 'Come', it opened to reveal Claudia and a younger girl. The younger girl carried a tray of food. Soft rolls, a pot of coffee.

'Contessa, the conte asked me to bring you breakfast at this time. Are you ready, Contessa?'

'Yes, thank you, Claudia.'

Glad that she had slipped into her robe, she sat up in bed to accept the tray.

'There is word from the conte too; he says he will meet you at noon, at the port. You will kindly take yourself there; the car is parked outside the door. You will need a small overnight bag. Shall I pack it for you?'

'An overnight bag? I don't suppose the conte said where we are going.'

'No, Contessa, but to the mainland. I know because you are to meet the boat at the jetty. He sent word; I did not see the conte himself.'

'Fine,' and then to herself, she murmured, but why the overnight bag?

It was intriguing. What should she pack? Red satin, perhaps? She smiled happily to herself.

There was a lightness about her – she felt like running, dancing singing . . . Luca . . . Luca was in her heart, now she remembered how she felt about him, how he made her feel.

Yet there had been times when . . . but what was it? Why was there a cloud now skimming across her heart . . . what had he done to her that made that shiver come?

'Go away sadness,' she murmured. 'I need to be happy; when I am happy I remember things. . . .'

She dressed in smart casuals, beautifully cut navy trousers and a dark mustard coloured cashmere sweater. There was a blazer on a hanger and she took that, slipping into it. Nautical but smart, she thought, before slipping into a pair of flat navy shoes. In the overnight bag she packed her nightdress, bag of toiletries and, on top, wrapped in tissue, a smart dress for evening wear. That and clean lingerie were really all she needed.

I pack well, she thought, I am used to it. It came as a surprise that little statement and for a moment she sat on the bed and explored it. She had accompanied Tony to Europe on many occasions. Sometimes she had gone ahead. There were times when she packed for him too. His wife preferred to live in the country and Tony lived alone in London. Was that living alone in the city the thing that brought about the end of his career? Perhaps it was something even more damaging. Tony, she recalled, had made a lot of enemies. Yet he was not a bad man, just arrogant at times. However, he did very well by his constituents. That she knew. It was why she had put up with him.

Sitting in the little Fiat, she hesitated. This would be her first time driving since she had arrived. Did she even know the way? Of course, down the drive, turn left, go through the village and right across the square, up the hill and down the other side, there, barely fifteen minutes away was the actual port. There was the harbour, with the shops and cafés circling the bay. They would be quiet this time of year but in the summer it was a hive of industry.

Turning the ignition, she fired up the little car, pushed it into gear and set off smoothly down the drive. The huge gates were thrown back – unusual that, for they were usually closed. It would be Luca, he would have asked Guido to leave them open for her. Parking on the road, she went back and pulled the huge gates to.

The launch was tied up by the quay and after sliding the Fiat into a parking space she walked eagerly across. Hoping it was not Antonio taking them, she felt relief when she saw that it was someone else. Someone she did not know. He was a man who was not very tall but thickset and looked as if he enjoyed working out with weights.

'Contessa,' he said, politely inclining his head and offering his hand to assist her on board.

She managed to embark elegantly, although the boat gave a little lurch and she soon heard the engine throbbing away. The gangplank was up and the boat was moving out into the bay before she asked, 'Where is the Conte?'

'I am sorry that you feel that way,' Rosa said. She held her features in check but could feel her lips tremble with inner fury. 'I thought that would never happen. You gave me assurance it would not happen.'

'Did I?' Luca asked.

'After what she did, you said you could never forgive her.'

'Did I ever say those *actual* words?'

Rosa shrugged. He was no fool. 'Not exactly.'

'Like Renata and my brother and his wife, you *assumed*. The truth was I could not forgive myself for not seeing how bad she was feeling. I ignored all the signs.'

Rosa stared at him and wondered how she had ever believed that she had him in her fist. He had taken her out to dinner parties, he had invited her to be his hostess and on two occasions she had travelled with him, but he had never touched her passionately. He maintained their friendship and their business ties but never had he allowed himself to be her lover. A kiss more friendly than emotional and that was it. Yet she had persevered, believing that in the end she would win what she had long desired. Luca, of course, but more importantly, the name he could give to her . . . Contessa, the power, and now the money as well – that would be pleasurable too, and would enable her to end her business adventure. That was becoming far too precarious and threatening. Her fellow travellers in business would also not be delighted by this turn of events. Alva was not a woman who would let things go; she was a curious little cat and was not afraid to voice what she felt. However, now it seemed that not only was *she* back but she was once more working her magic over the conte. Rosa had been sure she would succeed with him. They would not be best pleased when they found out *she* had failed.

'I'm sorry if I gave you the wrong idea, Rosa. We have been friends a long time and I would not—'

She put her hand up and smiled. 'No need to say it, Luca. I understand. But are you not just a little afraid that she—'

He cut off her words brutally, his anger clear as he barked, 'Do not dare to judge her or to interfere with me, Rosa. We are friends, but only up to a point. I will not have you making these dangerous suggestions.'

Crossing to him, she linked an arm through his. 'Luca, forgive me. I was presumptuous.' There was something so cold and cruel about him in that moment that she felt a shiver run along the length of her spine. Luca had always hated to be contradicted about *anything* – and his relationship with the Englishwoman in particular. 'But we can still have lunch, it is all arranged, that will be not be too onerous for you?'

'Of course not, Rosa. I just wanted to – as the English are fond of saying – lay my cards on the table. Let you know that there is a strong possibility that Alva may be staying. . . .'

She murmured, 'And Renata?'

He inclined his head, giving the broad hint that he would not discuss his daughter with her. Fool! He did not realize that the moment he had gone she would be on the telephone to someone who could stir the girl up to make trouble and that the lonely girl had been groomed to take a specific stand.

The telephone rang out, just as they were sitting down on the loggia for lunch. Excusing herself, Rosa went and answered it.

Alone, Luca mused over matters, he had told Rosa that he would no longer be seeing her as he used to. He wanted to spend more time with his wife, but as yet he had not said anything to his wife. Perhaps she would not like the idea of staying with him? Yet he would try. Divorce was not something that he relished anyway and he and Alva, they shared so much. Even should her memory not return he felt certain they could recapture some of what had been before. As to the rest, that could be sorted out. She was still in love with him, he was certain. He smiled, oh yes, he was certain of that.

When Rosa came back her colour was heightened. Her eyes sparkling, as if she were excited about something.

'Is everything all right?' Luca asked.

'Of course, everything is wonderful, Luca. For you at least . . . but my dear, will you require to renegotiate my lease? That was my lawyer on the telephone; he reminded me that my lease is up next April. It is not too far away.'

'There is nothing to renegotiate, Rosa, I am happy with the terms you have now, if you are?'

'Oh yes, of course,' she smiled at him. 'When I first came here Renata was a baby and you had Silvia. I remember when I came to the island and thought I had found paradise. I never realized that I would be living here for a good part of the year.'

'We've been friends a long time, Rosa, and I hope we will continue with that friendship. I appreciate how wonderful you have been to Renata, especially after her mother died. Losing her mother at such a tender age would have been traumatic for any girl but the circumstances. . . .' He shuddered. 'Her being there, in the car. . . .'

'I know how bad it was, Luca. I tried to be a kindly aunt to her. At such times a girl needs a woman's hand to hold. But you were wonderful too, Luca, suppressing your own pain to deal with Renata's.'

Luca looked away from her – she noted it through narrow eyes. Ah yes, she knew what he had felt when his wife had died and that he still felt a little guilty about it!

'But let us toast to our friendship, Luca, long may we share it.'

Later, in Rosa's beautifully appointed sitting-room, he surreptitiously glanced at his watch. Alva would wonder where he was. He had left a note on the table in the sunroom but he had said he would be home by four. Now it was past that hour, night was drawing in fast.

Rosa's rented villa was on the other, less populated part of the island. It stood high on a cliff overlooking the bay. It was perfect with splendid views; in fact, he realized wryly, nicer views than those at the palazzo.

The villa had been built by his grandfather – ostensibly to house his mistress – ironic that he then should rent it to a woman he had been tempted to have occupy that position in *his* life. Even odder that he had not done anything about it – but he could not analyse why that was so. He preferred to keep his reasons buried. It was safer that way.

It was dark as he drove back to the palazzo. There were no lights on the twisting road and he had his foot on the brake for most of the journey. This was where his first wife had driven off the road. He shuddered still when he thought of it. Beautiful and wilful Silvia, the woman he had married because it was expected of him. He had been nineteen at the time. At that age in his society you did not argue with your father. Although they too had had an attraction at some time, the marriage had not been happy or unhappy; it had been a marriage where both followed their lives. Silvia had been a talented artist and he had never objected to her pursuing her career. Renata was lucky to be alive, for the car had bounced down that steep tree-covered hillside like a toy car. How Renata had lived he would never know.

Once down from the hills, he speeded along the coast road, only slowing to go around the square, but once he hit the road to his home, he put on some speed. He was eager to see her, to talk to her. . . .

Inside the palazzo it was very quiet. The light illuminated the large hall; he went across it and down the passageway that led to the sunroom. There were no lights on, he turned on a light. His note had gone.

Quickly, he went back out, running up the stairs, then along the gallery to his wife's bedroom. Remembering her admonition of two nights ago, he knocked on the door. Pressing an ear to the panel he could hear nothing. Slowly, he opened the door. The room was in darkness, no light came from the bathroom, and it was obvious she was not there.

Instead of calling on the downstairs phone he took to the stairs once more. This time he went to the library, here there was light, just from a table lamp. Realizing he could not go from room to room, he went to the kitchen. If anyone knew where she was hiding herself, it would be Claudia.

'Conte!' Claudia whirled around as he entered. The cook was also there, she was sitting in her chair, knitting; there was no sign of food preparation for their evening meal. Usually at this time the kitchen was a hive of activity and lots of chatter and the clattering of pans.

'Conte, I am so sorry – you were not expected.' The woman

stood, bobbing a little, perhaps disturbed by his look of consternation.

'What do you mean? Not expected.'

'But you sent word, Conte, to the contessa to go to the launch, to take an overnight bag; we thought' – she looked over her shoulder – 'that you had gone to the mainland for a night,' she shrugged, 'or somewhere else.'

'What do you mean?' he repeated.

CHAPTER FIVE

APPREHENSION was slow in dawning. Not knowing the man who was taking her to the mainland, she had gone to sit in the stern, watching the island go further away from her. Turning her head she noticed that instead of going directly across the bay, the quickest route and the one that Antonio had taken, the boat had swung in a wide arc and was actually following the coast rather than going directly to the port.

Her mouth opened, she was about to question him when sense prevailed. There was something odd about him and about the journey.

Standing, she made her way towards the hatch; he was going at a far faster rate of knots than last time she had crossed, the sway of the boat caused her to be a little unsteady.

'Contessa?' He asked as he saw her.

She smiled. 'I need to go below,' she murmured.

He offered no opposition. Obviously, he did not fear that she was suspicious about him, yet why should she be feeling like that? Perhaps he liked to make the journey longer? This boat was certainly a perfect boy's toy. Nevertheless, apprehension was there. She had long learned that such feelings should not be ignored.

In the cabin she looked around, crossing to a set of drawers. Opening them, she looked for something – some implement that would offer her protection should she need it. There was nothing. On the far side there was a chart table; on the top of some charts were a divider and some projectors. The divider had a sharp pointed end like a dart. It would be difficult to hurt someone badly with it, but it would cause some damage, especially if she used it at a vulnerable spot.

Grabbing it, she put it in the pocket of her blazer before climbing up on deck.

Her heart plummeted, they had sped across the bay so fast, far away from the town, and the mainland was a blur now. She knew that her instinct was right. Something was terribly wrong.

Alva asked. 'Where are we going?'

The man turned and looked at her, then looked away.

'How dare you ignore me!' she said. Putting on an imperious manner to cover her fear was not all that difficult. She had seen how her husband could do just that.

'Shut up,' he said, pushing her. The boat swayed under her feet, she grabbed a rail steadying herself. The engine slowed to a stop, the boat bobbed but gently on the undulating sea.

'You should really have stayed away, Contessa. . . .'

He came towards her. Sliding her hand out of her pocket she clasped the divider in her right hand, hiding it at her side. When he reached her, he took hold of her arm, the left. In his right hand he had something . . . it was a syringe. Urgently, her hand shot out. His chinos were thin; she aimed for the soft spot at the top of his thigh, it made little impact, other than to startle him. Before he could move she raised her hand aiming for his face, it made contact with his cheek, perforating it only as a pin prick.

Struggling to hold her caused the boat to pitch and rock. She was light but fit now, and wriggled like an eel. Her hand, as the divider slipped from her fingers, went to the back of his head, pulling hard on his longish hair, her foot finding his, grinding against his toes. He had to drop the syringe to try to pull her hand out of his hair, his left arm went up around her throat, trying to press close to her windpipe . . . she moved violently, causing the boat to rock even more. He lost balance, just for a second having to steady himself and in that second without a thought of anything, she scrambled on the seat and leapt from the boat.

The water took her, down . . . dragging at her . . . wanting to suck her to its sandy bottom.

Who was the man? Had they seen him before? The conte was furious. Claudia and the cook cowered in front of him, and then Claudia remembered the note and went into the pockets of her apron. It simply stated: *'Ask the contessa to go to the launch, tell her to bring an overnight bag. We are going to the mainland. L.M.'*

The writing was a good facsimile of his own – not perfect and would be recognized by anyone who really knew him as a forgery – but Claudia, he had to admit, was not the brightest when it came to analysis of any kind. It was also unlikely that Alva would remember what his writing looked like, she barely remembered *him*.

He swore but not at them any more, more at the whole sick mess. Going to the telephone he called someone he thought might know something about it. They drew a blank, advising him to call the police.

The police had a station at the quayside and by looking out of the window they could see if the launch was there. It was not at its berth, they confirmed immediately.

'I think my wife has been kidnapped!' He said the words, feeling inside him a terrible dread. This kind of thing happened on the mainland . . . but not here! Not on his safe little island where everyone looked out for everyone else.

'Conte, we will send out a police launch at once,' the officer assured him.

'*Grazi* . . . I will take my helicopter as well. . . .'

'Conte, I would strongly advise against it – it might be better if you wait, there could be contact . . . you must stay by the telephone.'

'I can't do that!'

The police officer did not argue. You did not argue with the conte if his mind were made up. 'If you insist, conte, then it must be.'

On his way to the helipad he called Antonio. Antonio would fly the machine and he could look out.

Four pairs of eyes were better than two.

'Are you sure something has happened?' Antonio asked him. 'If the contessa is ill again it might be that she has gone away of her own accord.'

'And she would send a letter from me telling her to meet me? I doubt she would be so devious. Besides, the contessa is not ill any more.'

Antonio turned the helicopter around, dipping over the ocean. There was the passenger ferry crossing and he saw the police launch but there was no sign of another boat in the vicinity.

'The contessa has regained her memory?'

'Not entirely.' Luca threw a look in Antonio's direction. He seemed remarkably calm. 'I hope you don't know anything about it!' he snapped.

'Of course not,' Antonio said. 'Why would you think that?'

'I don't know what to think!'

He had been unkind at times to Alva. He had not understood enough the way Alva had felt and he admitted now that he had expected too much of her and of Renata. Sick with worry now he saw so many things more clearly. Yet he knew that Alva also had made a nuisance of herself, interfering where it was not necessary for her to do so. She had played a part in making him angry but then he realized she would not be Alva without that stubborn streak. He should have realized that before allowing himself to fall in love with her!

'Go around the point,' he said.

'But there is nothing out there,' Antonio murmured.

'Precisely. I really hope Antonio that you do not know anything about this!'

'I assure you, Conte I do not. I swear to you.'

'Very well, then go where I say.'

Her jacket was dragging her down once more; when she surfaced she could not see the boat. It took a long time and a surprising amount of energy to pull the jacket off. She had managed to kick off her shoes and tried to float and lie still for a moment. The waves were lapping and fortunately there was barely any wind.

Land was far away in the distance. She knew she would never swim that far – she was a good swimmer but it would be impossible. Laboriously, she pulled off her trousers, treading water. They were easier to remove than her jacket had been.

The thought that she would drown dawned on her slowly. It was growing dark, the sea would get colder. *I went through everything for this?* she thought, and then felt an overwhelming sense of self-pity.

Why? What had happened? Did someone want her dead? But there was no reason . . . there could not be a reason, unless Luca . . . if Luca wanted her dead there had to be something she had that he wanted. It was ridiculous even to think that.

She struck out with a slow breast stroke. That motion would halve the energy required. If she was going to die she was not just going to give up, she was made of stronger stuff than that.

Now there was nothing in front of her but blackness. The mainland that had seemed far away had now disappeared. It had to be a remote part of the coastal strip because there were no lights. Where would that be. . . ? She had no idea. Pushing herself forward she thought of her life, the blank canvas that her life had become. I remember Luca, she thought, our meeting, our time at Juan la Pins . . . there was nothing else.

Something slimy slid between her legs, a large fish . . . she panicked, rushing into a vigorous crawl, thinking of sharks – but she was not in shark infested waters. There was nothing to fear but the sea itself. . . .

Where was the boat? Was she going the right way? Was she turning in circles?

The waves mounted, rushing around her, pushing her to one side as if she were in a rip current. She was tossed about, the rough brush of the sea bruising against her legs.

There was sound . . . a steady thrumming echoing the thud of her heart. She tried to see, turning frantically in the water, she could be in the way of a ship, a huge cruise liner, a speedboat, the man looking for her. If she cried out, if by a miracle someone heard her and if it were him, he would kill her anyway and she realized with a terrible sadness, that she would rather drown than that. . . .

There was a light now; she saw it, way to the left of her . . . a craft of some kind, not large. It was heading out to sea, away from her . . . there was a gantry, it was a fishing boat. Then behind it another one . . . and another . . . the wash was growing more violent, apart from the lights of the boats there was no light. It would be impossible for them to see her, and, because of the throbbing engines, they would not hear her either.

Quickly she headed into the pitching waves . . . they tossed her about like a cork, pulling her back, there was no way she could swim against it . . . she was too tired, there were too many boats. . . .

She cried out, her voice now, coated with salt, was no more than a croak. Rescue was there but it would be impossible. She even heard voices in the dark . . . joking, laughter . . . a name or two '*Giovanni . . . Vincente*.'

'We must go home now, Conte. . . .' He heard Antonio's voice above the din of the helicopter. It was pitch black, the sea below a large empty mass of water. No boats . . . nothing.

'Go around once more,' he said coldly.

'But Conte. . . .'

'Do as I say!'

His voice, full of authority and arrogance echoed back to him. Damn the man, but Antonio took things too far some of the time. He determined that one of these days he would do something about it. However, it was good advice, as had the suggestion of the policeman been good sense – he should wait for a call. That was what was important. The police knew how to handle a kidnapping, whereas he had no idea. . . .

He had almost decided to tell Antonio to turn back when he saw lights below, lots of lights.

'What is that?'

'It is the fishing fleet going to Maria Santa. . . .'

'Of course.' The Conte took up the radio, calling the police . . . had they thought to ask the fishing fleet to look out for his boat. . . .

Of course they had. Each captain had been instructed and promised to have a look out on deck.

'Perhaps—' His heart stilled and when it started to race once more he felt momentarily dizzy. His head was spinning. 'Maybe she is not in the boat. . . .'

Antonio cast him a look.

He grabbed the radio and called up the police.

'Conte,' the policeman said, 'they would not do that, they want money, it is too soon. . . .'

'I know, I know . . . but please indulge me.'

If she got trapped in the wake she knew she could not survive. Exhausted, her body was being tossed about like so much flotsam, twice she dipped under the water. Images were flashing like a flickering film into her mind. *Buildings?* how stupid was it to be seeing buildings in her mind when she was far from terra firma. A large elegant Queen Anne building that she recognized as her school. A large Victorian house that was the home of her parents. She did not see her mother and father, just the building and recognized it as her home before they died.

'Where is the money?' the question flew into her mind and stayed there like a fluttering bird. This was madness, she tried to concentrate on staying afloat but it was too hard. Just as she thought it would be best just to give in, a blinding light settled on her, hurting her eyes.

There were excited cries . . . Italian voices, they sounded hysterical. Weakly she raised a hand. Did she call out? She could not be sure. The choppy waves stilled, almost as if someone had breathed on them. There was silence and the thrum of engines had stilled. She floated on to her back, moving her fingers to keep herself afloat. The light stayed.

'Contessa. . . .' A voice close by . . . hands, rough wonderful hands hauling her up into a life raft. The men all smelt of fish, she had been going the wrong way, she realized as one put his jacket around her, they were not going from port but heading to it.

Once she was hauled on the deck of the trawler, she collapsed. Rough hands rubbed her back, stimulating the blood flow. Her teeth were chattering but even against this the throbbing of the engines as the boat headed for port was music to her ears.

It was madness at the harbour. There were policemen and an ambulance, crowds of people filling the street; it was as if they all had come tumbling out of their homes to see what was going on. It is not for me, she thought, they have come out because the boats are back, they are here to greet their men. . . .

Some warming stuff was wrapped around her; it looked like tinfoil but gave out a lot of heat. The men struggled against the mob with the stretcher, crying out excitedly for more room. Then the door of the ambulance slammed shut as she was laid on the bed and they set off, sirens blazing into the dark of night.

She felt herself falling to sleep. 'Don't sleep, Contessa,' the man at her side urged, he gave her a warming drink . . . someone put a needle in her arm.

'Luca,' she murmured.

'He will be at the hospital,' the man said, 'very soon, Contessa.'

Her eyes hurt. She opened them and they burned. Worst of all her lips felt so swollen and sore and dry. She had slept, falling deep into nothingness. Now it was still dark; a very soft light burned at the far side of the room. A shape loomed by the window, peering out of the slatted blinds two fingers holding the slats apart.

Where was she? She shifted slightly, feeling the crispness of sheets against her legs. Peeling open her eyes once more she peered through the dimness. A room, not too big; there was a rail at the foot of the bed. A hospital bed. Her heart thudded softly against her ribs, she was safe. No one could harm her here, could they?

The man had turned, moving softly across the room. The shadows falling from him showed her it was Luca.

'Alva,' he lowered himself on to the bed, taking up her hand in his. His hand felt warm and strong against her own. 'Alva,' he murmured again, brushing back the hair from her face. 'Let me. . . .' He took up a stick of some kind and smoothed it across her salt encrusted lips. It soothed and cooled. 'How are you, *cara mia*?'

She tried to speak but the words sounded like those of an angry frog.

He smiled. 'Just nod your head, do you feel better?'

She nodded.

'I want to take you home, to Santa Catarina.'

He saw a flicker in her eyes, recognized it as fear, and raised her hand to his lips.

'Nothing will ever happen to you again, I will protect you.'

She wanted to say you can't, no one can protect me entirely. Things keep happening and I don't know why. The hit and run in London. Her falling down the stairs . . . was that really an accident? Now this – a man on the boat, a syringe in his hand.

Raising her hand she mimed paper and pencil. He went away and was soon back, accompanied by a white-coated doctor.

The *dottore* started to fuss and take her temperature, feel her forehead, check her pulse. Impatience needed to be controlled. If she made a fuss it could be misconstrued – she was suspicious of hospitals, did not trust that they would let her leave. Her mind was a jumble of confused thoughts.

Eventually he left, leaving Luca to hand her the pencil and paper. 'I am sorry about that, I met him in the corridor and I foolishly told him you were awake.'

Nodding to let him know she understood, she concentrated on writing words on the pad. He waited until she had finished before he looked at what she was writing. It was a description of the man who had taken the launch, the man who had tried to kill her. All this she put down in broken, unpunctuated sentences.

'I understand,' Luca said. 'And the police will come and talk to you. Now you must have something to drink. Perhaps a little food. You have to rest. Tomorrow I want to take you home if they will let me, you will come?'

She wrote on the pad. *'I want to get out of here!'*

'You will, I promise.' He leaned over, very gently kissing her cheek. 'Oh, my darling, if I had lost you. . . .'

Her heart, even weak as she was, gave a pleasant lurch. He seemed so distressed. Could it be that he cared for her?

She lay back against the pillows, tired by the exertion of trying to get everything down on paper. Luca took up her hand once more and held it until her eyes fluttered to a close.

In the end she spent five days in the hospital. They were adamant, there were things to look for, and because of her previous accident they had to be extra vigilant. Not even for the conte would they do something so irresponsible as to allow their patient to leave. If she insisted on signing herself out there was nothing they could do, but . . . and that 'but' was couched in such a threatening tone, that Alva acquiesced. She would stay and give them what they wanted.

When the door opened and Luca came to visit it was alarming to see that there was a policeman on the door. They, too, had been vigilant and very, very caring. They sent a sketch artist and then went away only to return later with some mug shots. The man was not amongst them. He was not in the system.

'I don't know why,' she murmured, 'but I think perhaps he was not Italian. Oh, he spoke good Italian but there was a faint accent . . . very, slight. . . .'

'Albanian perhaps, or from Istria . . . he could be Swiss. . . ?'

'Maybe the latter, it was so slight as to be hardly noticeable but now that I concentrate I hear it. I did not exactly have a conversation with him but I remember he swore at me and there was a different language from Italian there . . . foreign swearwords, just one or two. . . .'

They went away again, presumably to liaise with Interpol.

The launch had been found, wrecked on a remote beach, partly burned out. 'He did not make a good job of the fire; probably he did not have time. *Figlio di puttana*!' Luca uttered, slamming his fist into the palm of his hand. Forensics was going over it and there were fingerprints but again, nothing on the system. Whoever this man was he had not broken the law in Italy . . . but perhaps somewhere else.

'He wanted to kill me,' she said one day to Luca as he sat on the bed.

'What? No, he wanted to kidnap you. He wanted money for you, who would want to kill you?'

'I don't know.' Was this to be it again, was she not going to believed yet again. She looked up at Luca, studying his face. There were lines of worry at his mouth. 'He tried to choke me, he said I would die. It wasn't a kidnap. He had a syringe, he was going to drug me, or worse. . . .'

'But why? It makes no sense. I would have paid a ransom to have you back.'

'What did he say? I fought with him and he said something,' she put her fingertips to her forehead and massaged her temples. 'Something about I should have stayed away. . . .' Helplessly she looked at her husband. 'As if someone did not want me to be with you. Did not want me back at the island.'

Renata? The name flew into her mind . . . Renata hated her but surely not that much. No, it would not be Renata, she must not think that, must not give the impression that she even suspected Luca's daughter of wanting her dead.

'There is no one that would feel that way. I know that Renata is upset that we may be together but she is not part of this.'

She lied, the lie slid off her tongue and she hated herself. 'No, I know that . . . but there has to be something else. And maybe it is nothing to do with you and me but to do with something in my past that I don't remember. When I was in the water I thought about money, I thought, "what happened to the money", but what money was it?'

'I don't know what that could be, *cara* but there could be something neither of us knows about. The accident in London, the hit and run. . . .'

'Perhaps I knew something about some missing money. Do you think it could be to do with Tony?'

'Tony? Antonio you mean?'

'No, Tony Laker, the man I worked for.'

'Tony, you remember his name? Ah, but it will be from our discussion.'

'No, I don't think so . . . only a day or so ago it came to me quite naturally. You said he was disgraced? Could it be to do with that?'

Luca stared into her eyes. 'After all this time? Unlikely, although he was a slippery character.'

'Well how was he disgraced?'

'Too friendly with someone who was into shady deals; he had received a lot of gifts from this person, and then there was the girl . . . young, you know the kind of thing. Presenting himself as a family man but all the time he had this slip of a girl on the side.'

'Miranda.' The name came from no where. 'Lots of red hair and gorgeous. . . .'

'You remember!'

'Yes I do, just now. A very posh girl but—'

'I am sorry?'

'You know, good family, right schools and connections, she modelled a bit. Had everything going for her on the outside but a bit of a dimwit otherwise.'

He laughed softly. 'You have a fine way of summing people up, *cara* – still, I don't know why I am laughing because none of this is funny.'

'The Miranda affair was funny. Even Tony's wife thought it ridiculous. If it had not had so much publicity I think she would have stood by him but she just thought, "What the hell, I don't want to do this anymore". However, I think it was more to do with the other thing . . . the one you were telling me about. This bloke he was in cahoots with. I don't remember his name. If I ever knew it. Surely it can't be anything to do with that? I mean, that *is* a blast from the past. If I knew anything then, they would have acted on it at the time.'

'True . . . but it was after we were married that everything went wrong for Tony. In fact it was while. . . .'

'Yes?' She took up his hand, holding on to it. 'Tell me . . . let's not have secrets.'

'It happened while you were in hospital.'

'My breakdown . . . that time?'

'Yes. This is the first time we have discussed it because you left me. . . .'

'You didn't come after me?'

He had the grace to turn his head away, then, making up his mind, turned to face her. 'Things were said, it was impossible to go back from them.'

'I said things to you, rather than you to me?'

'More or less. Then you left the hospital and I did not know where you had gone. You had not even discharged yourself. You just walked out.'

'So it wasn't a secure unit?'

'Alva, of course it was not. It was a private clinic.'

'Good. I thought you had me banged up like the wife in the attic.'

He stared at her for a moment but seeing the twinkle in her eye merely smiled. 'I am not Mr Rochester,' he murmured. 'You see, I do listen to you, Alva, and I know that is your favourite book.'

Later, when Luca had left for the hotel where he was staying, she lay in bed listening to the soft sounds of the hospital. A squeak of a trolley being pushed along the corridor, its wheels swishing along the thick floor covering. A cough somewhere, the laugh of a couple of nurses.

It was late, the light in the corridor was dimmed, and she knew the guard had changed. The night one was called Giuseppe and she knew that one of the nurses was rather sweet on him because she had heard them talking. He did not seem over keen but she was a game girl and kept trying.

All these irrelevant thoughts drifted in and out of her mind. She had to concentrate really hard not to relive those moments on the boat, or the time in the sea.

It had seemed hours but it was not even an hour. If the fishing fleet had not found her she knew she would have drowned. She had been in the darkness swimming away from the shore. How could she have done that . . . why had she not looked for the North Star which was a guiding light, ah . . . she knew little about the stars and the heavens. Had she seen the North Star it was unlikely she would have recalled what it was telling her.

Luca. He came to her, filling her senses with wonder. Just why had she said things that had made it impossible for him to come and find her? He said she would remember and he did not want to go over it with her. Not now, maybe in the future if she did not remember. She knew he meant it for her own good but in what he told her might lie some clues as to why she had done that and, more importantly, why she had twice been in situations that had left her close to death.

The room smelled delicious, it was full of flowers. They were from Luca and from the servants. There was a bunch of pale cream roses from Rosa d'Casta, which was kind – even though she did not like the woman it had been thoughtful of her. Perhaps she had misjudged her on their first meeting. After all, what had the woman done that was so terrible? She had tried to monopolize Luca but it was to her that Luca came, and who could blame Rosa anyway? Luca was the kind of man a lot of women would take a strong fancy to, and she had to be used to that. Besides, she was not the jealous type.

Even more surprising than the flowers from Rosa was the delicious basket of fruit that came from Renata. At first she had thought that Luca had ordered it but on checking she found the order had come from Rome. She had asked one of the nurses to find out. It had been a ridiculous enterprise and came from someone with too many idle hours, because when he had seen it Luca had been utterly surprised.

'My goodness, my daughter has not forgotten her good manners after all!'

'It's kind of her, Luca and if you give me her address I will write and tell her so.'

Now she was ready to leave; she said nothing about how frail she felt, afraid that her release from the hospital would be delayed if anyone knew how she truly felt. Gladly she held on to Luca's arm, and held him tightly. It was cold outside; she shivered, tugging the cashmere cardigan closer to her. Once inside the car, Luca tucked a warm blanket around her. Dark clouds roared across the sky and as they drove to the heliport light spots of rain dusted the windshield.

'I have a new launch but I thought the helicopter would be quicker. I want you home – you will be safe there.'

'Safe from what?' She clasped his hand. 'Don't you think it's over?'

'Do you?'

She shook her head. She thought of the freedom that she loved, riding down to the beach, strolling into town, taking the launch to the mainland, was all this at an end because someone thought she knew *something*?

In the past she had been miserable and unhappy, Luca said she had been very depressed when she was pregnant. She thought she must have been hell to live with. Whatever had made her that way, she was determined it would not happen again. It could have been the pregnancy and her feeling ill with it, but it could have been this terrible thing that she knew about weighing on her mind. 'I'm not going to give into fear, Luca, I want to enjoy my life, I want to enjoy—' She stopped, she had been going to say 'you', but perhaps that would be a step too far. She recalled only too well what he had said at the hospital. He had said '*that we may be together*,' there had been no surety in that statement. He had had to clarify it.

'Yes?'

'Just living.'

'You will be safe on my island,' he assured her. 'There will be no more mystery notes from me. I bought you a new mobile telephone. If you don't hear from me that we will meet somewhere you will not go. I have a new man working for me now. You will meet him but he won't be obtrusive around you. I need you to liaise with him if you are going anywhere – please do this for me?'

'Of course. I don't relish another experience like that last one,' she smiled up at him.

'I promise not to be stubborn and stupid about it.'

'Good. I know that you liked Maryanne and Curtis Trevor and so I've invited them for a long weekend. . . .'

'Lovely,' she said, relishing the idea of the company of the American couple.

'But I cannot let them film – I explained to them and they

understand. It would bring too many strangers to the island and I cannot risk it.'

'That's a shame. I'm sorry I caused that but I do understand your reasoning. I only hope *they* do.'

'Of course they do. Especially since I have suggested somewhere else where there will be no problem.'

CHAPTER SIX

HER minder was called Carlo. He was a large, solidly built man, especially for an Italian, and he had fair hair and light blue eyes. He came from the north, Luca explained. There was probably some Teutonic ancestry if one looked far back.

He certainly looked like a man who could handle any situation. He spoke good English too, but with a slight American accent. He explained that he had lived in the States for a short time. She thought she could trust him. Her feelings about Carlo were very different from her feelings for Antonio; she could still not get over her feeling of loathing when she looked at the man. Yet he did nothing really to alarm her. In fact he had been very solicitous of her well-being when he flew them back to the island from the hospital.

'You won't be with me all the time,' she murmured.

'If I am you won't be aware of it, Contessa,' Carlo assured.

'Well,' she smiled up at him, lowering her lashes in the hope of hiding her worries.

'It should work OK . . . I'll try to be co-operative.'

And later when she and Luca were alone she said, 'I quite like him.'

'That's good, he comes highly recommended.'

Looking across at Luca she saw he still seemed worried.

Now and again he gave her a long penetrating stare when he thought she was not aware of it. Deep inside him he still thinks that I tried to commit suicide and worse ... that I wanted to kill the child he put inside me. Sadly, she turned to walk away, only hesitating as she reached the door that let out into the hall. Turning back she caught him watching her once more, weighing her, his hands curled into fists as if he had to control himself, to stop himself from doing something or saying something . . . but what?

'What time do the Trevors' arrive tomorrow?' she asked. She knew but felt she needed an excuse for her abrupt turn around.

'After lunch. Curtis has a meeting.'

'I'd like to plan dinner, is that all right?'

'Of course, Alva, this is your home.'

Is it? The words bounced into her mind. You made love to me, we came together with such joy but now we are back where we started. There is a distance between us. Perhaps it will always be there. The sex was good, she remembered his hurtful words, and doubtless it would always be, but in-between times there was a void, and in spite of what had happened to her it would never be filled. The terrible birth and death of their child was in his head and he could never let go of the thought that it was all her doing.

'But who would want to hurt you?' Maryanne asked, curling her arm around Alva's. 'I thought it a kidnapping. I had no idea this man had tried to kill you!'

'I don't know . . . was it a kidnapping gone wrong? He had his hands at my throat, he had a syringe and it was I who jumped from the boat. Maybe he just wanted me docile.' She shook her head. 'It was all so fast; I am sure, and yet when you ask that, it makes me doubt myself.'

'No, don't doubt what happened to you. You know better

than anyone else. It just seems preposterous that someone would want you dead. Ransom I can understand, but to want to murder you. Why? But of course you don't know why because you can't remember – God, Alva, how are you standing it?'

'I think there's a good bit of iron in me. I'm fearful yet I won't give into it. I am not going to lock myself away.'

'You don't think someone wants you out of the way because of Luca?'

'No. I don't see anyone wanting to kill me that badly. I mean, who wants me out of the way? – just Renata and even she wouldn't plan to kill me. She hates me, but it is a *girl* thing with her. It isn't me personally, she would be the same to anyone who married her father.'

They reached the cabanas and went inside to change into swimsuits. The air was not too warm but the pool was heated and Maryanne had said a swim was just what she needed. A weak sun caused the green-blue water to sparkle a little, and once she slid her body into it, the warmth engulfed Alva.

They swam side by side, doing a slow breaststroke, talking and laughing. It reminded Alva of other times but she could not see who the other person was. She remembered doing just that, at an indoor pool swimming alongside someone whose company she enjoyed.

A dusky cloud slid across the patch of blue, bringing with it a spurt of soft rain. The women laughed but carried on swimming and talking. One of the maids came out bearing a tray of coffee things. The soft breeze wafted the aroma of freshly brewed coffee across to them.

'That smells good to me, one more lap and I'm out of here.'

'Me too!' Alva agreed.

But in the end she did two more. Maryanne was already wrapped in a thick toweling robe before she pulled herself out of the pool.

'We have to be mad!' Alva said.

'I know, but isn't it fun? I remember once when Curtis and I were in New Zealand. We went to this place where there were three hot pools to swim in, warm, very warm and warmer still, and it was pouring with rain but people were in there. Curtis wouldn't, California chicken I guess, but I was in there. You can't beat a Boston girl when it comes to stamina!'

'I'd have been in there with you. At school we had to swim all year round, and the pool was not heated. Why is it these places have to punish kids?' She asked lightheartedly.

'That's a memory,' Maryanne said gently.

'Yes, they do pop into my head now and then. Little bits of my past life.'

'It will all come back one day, I'm sure of it. But aren't you glad of those cold swims? It's certainly made you tough.'

'Yes, you're right. I guess that education I had has made me what I am. I won't let anyone get me down. Well—' She felt her eyes glaze over with unshed tears and, turning away, she chewed her lip for a moment. Something had once pushed her down into darkness, so far down that she had ended up in a psychiatric unit. Luca might dress it up as a private clinic, but that was what it was. But not any more. She unselfconsciously pushed back her shoulders and jerked up her chin. Whatever happened she would do battle with it, even if it broke her heart.

Sipping her coffee she felt oddly refreshed. Not just from the swim but from the company of this other woman. Maryanne was a new friend but a person that she felt she had known all her life. Incredible but it was there inside her, a feeling that this was a friendship that would be for keeps. Maryanne was someone with whom she could reveal all her uncertainties and with whom she could share the passing of Alessandro.

Later she took a long leisurely bath before dinner. She pinned up her hair and allowed herself the luxury of just lying in warm scented water. When she had finished there were warm fluffy towels to dry herself on, and with a huge bath towel wrapped around her she went to her wardrobe to look for something to wear.

A dark-green velvet pantsuit caught her eye and she selected that. The fitted jacket, with a mandarin collar, skimmed her body perfectly as did the pants. It was obviously an outfit she had when she had previously lived here.

Once dressed, she flicked a brush through her hair and was only slightly startled when she heard the door open. Through the mirror she saw the reflection of her husband.

He had been riding around the island with Curtis who was a keen horseman. Obviously it had done him the power of good, for he looked brighter than she had seen him looking for some time. In a white silk shirt and dark jacket and trousers he looked relaxed.

'I love that,' he nodded to the suit. 'It is a perfect match for your eyes.'

'Is it? I hadn't thought.'

'Of course you hadn't.'

Alva looked for sarcasm but there was none there. He meant it kindly.

'You have no vanity, Alva, which is what I liked about you.'

'Thank you,' she murmured.

'What did you do today?' he asked, going to sit on the ottoman.

She went through her day; he visibly shivered when she told him about their swim. 'It was fun – and I remembered about school, how they never heated the pool!'

'Good. You never told me that, or if you did I don't remember. I am sure being Italian I would remember your telling me about swimming in icy waters.'

'You don't think I am imagining it do you?' she asked anxiously.

'Of course not. It was not so important that you would share that with me. So, you enjoyed your day with Maryanne?'

For a moment she hesitated before answering, smoothing a finger over her eyebrow. Not wanting to sound foolish about how important this friendship seemed to be. Yet it was difficult to keep things from Luca. He had that way with him that drew things out of her. He had always had it, that warmth and charm that made confession easy.

'I like her very much. It's just as if I have found a true friend.'

'Good. Friendship is important. You had a lot of friends, Alva. But,' he hesitated wondering whether to go on. 'Your Christmas card list is huge . . . most of your girlfriends had married and had children by the time we met. They lived in different places, different countries even. There was a girl that you were close to. Chloe. . . .'

'Really?'

'You used to say that Chloe was your soulmate.'

'Really?' she asked again with more emphasis.

'She died. Cancer. We were going out together at the time and you were heartbroken.'

'Oh my God.' She sank on to the ottoman beside him. 'And I can't even remember Chloe.'

'You were at school together. She was a tiny girl, a will of a wisp you called her. She had lovely dark curls and laughing blue eyes. She lost her hair with the treatment . . . I remember your crying about that. Crying not for yourself but because it had upset her.'

'I wish I could remember. How could I forget someone that I loved?'

Luca took up her hand, turning it over he very gently kissed the palm. 'You forgot me too, so do not distress yourself about it. One day it will all come back to you.'

'Perhaps I don't want it all back, Luca; there have to be things that are best not remembered.'

'You have nothing in your past to be ashamed about. I am certain of that, Alva.'

'Except—' she caught the words, pulling them back. She had wanted to say what you believe I did to our child, but she would not go there with him. One day she might remember and have evidence to prove that she had not done anything wrong. Just one day it might all be revealed and then . . . then it would be over. His pain and his suffering would be burned away. He still felt guilty, believing that he had not done enough to support her through her terrible time. Yet instinctively she knew it was not his fault, and nor was it hers, there was something there and one day it would all come out.

'Luca, since I've been back from the hospital you haven't . . . I mean,' she felt her cheeks scorch; her hand, as she glanced at it, looked so small trapped in his. 'I need you, Luca; I need you to come to me. . . .'

He bent his head, capturing her ear in his mouth, very gently. It felt no more than the heartbeat of a butterfly but was nonetheless devastating.

'Then I will come, Alva. I did not know if you were well enough . . . I thought you needed lots of rest. . . .'

'I do.' Gathering her courage to her, chasing away the dark shadows deep inside her, she smiled up at him. 'But, Luca, there is rest and there is rest. . . .'

Alva awakened from a disturbed sleep. The silk sheets were wrapped around her body in a mummy-like hold. Gasping she fought herself free, and then found herself breathless.

What had happened? Where was she? It was still fairly dark but a chink of light crept in through the partly opened shutter.

She was alone. Of course! Luca was away. He had had to go

to the mainland on business and chose to travel there with Maryanne and Curtis Trevor. He would be gone for three days, he had said . . . while there he intended to take the opportunity to visit Renata in Rome.

It was too soon for her to see her stepdaughter. He had not asked her to accompany him and she had not tried to persuade him to let her do so. She was not afraid of being alone here, anyway, not with the strong and silent Carlo to look after her. However, there was *something* that had frightened her. Was it a dream? She struggled to a sitting position, pummelling the pillow and then leaning back, closing her eyes, searching her mind.

Something ominous and dark had wrapped itself around her heart. It was more than a lump of fear, it was even worse than depression. There was something lodged in her mind, but it was buried, yet during her restless night, it had come to her . . . in her sleep. No, it was not a dream . . . it was a memory.

Determinedly, she ticked off things in her mind. Was it to do with Tony her old boss . . . or was it a memory that she had shared with Chloe? She had been trying too hard to remember her friend, the girl with whom Luca said she had shared so much. However, Chloe was not there, not even a visual image of her friend came into her mind. It was not Chloe; anyway, it was hardly likely that if she remembered anything about Chloe it would frighten her. Sadness maybe but not fear, for Chloe had never brought harm to her, Alva was certain of that.

An image came to her now, beating against her closed lids. It was dark; there were long shadows of a summer night. Stillness, not a breath of wind, sultry heat. Luca was there. He was crossing the garden stealthily. It was obvious he did not want to be seen by anyone and he was coming from the shabby buildings close to the indoor pool. She was there, hiding, watching, her heart throbbing against the wall of her chest, waves of heat streaming against her skin. She felt terribly weak, almost as if she would faint. Something was going on in the building, something wrong. Fear and terror choked the breath from her. Luca was involved . . . *but in what?*

Exhausted, Alva slid down into the bed, wrapping the coverlet about her. It was a dream but if it was, why did it seem to be so real?

Later coaxing herself from bed, she showered and changed into fleecy sweat pants and matching hoodie. The maid had brought her coffee and warm rolls, she drank the coffee and picked at the roll but she was anxious to be outside.

There was no one around, the house seemed so silent but not ominously so. The clock in the hallway told her it was only ten o'clock, the servants were probably having their morning break. As if to prove her assumption, a tinkle of laughter drifted up from the kitchen. Once outside she walked swiftly to the disused buildings adjacent to the swimming pool.

At her touch the door swung open. The day outside was gloomy so there was not much light inside. The window frames were grey with dust. Brushing her hand along the wall she sought for the light switch and on finding it, clicked it on. The light flickered as if the bulb were about to go out, then it settled.

It was grim inside. The once beautiful tiles were chipped and grubby, scuffed with a hundred or more shoeprints. There was soil here and there. A sack of something or other had been chewed by vermin and spilled something on to the floor. Touching it she realized it was merely fertilizer and nothing sinister. In each and every corner, huge spiders' webs hung, rather beautiful in the light, thin and delicately spun but empty of any captive.

Moving deeper into the room she saw there were three

doors on the far side. Crossing to them she opened the first, it led down to a flight of stairs but it was dark, and a smell of rot and damp wafted up. The switch when she clicked it, did not light the bulb that precariously hung from a beam only slightly above her head. The stairs were stone and quite steep. There was no way she was going there to explore.

The other doors led only into storerooms, empty of anything but dust and an air of decay. Cold shivers ran down her spine and she backed away. She had to get out, she felt unable to breath, her throat had become constricted, it had to be the dust – she coughed but it brought no relief. Turning she collided with something solid; she stepped back, gasping, her back slamming into the rim of the door. She almost lost her balance and toppled down into the dark flight of stairs. A strong hand clasped her wrist.

'Contessa, are you all right?'

Weakly she looked up at last. It was Carlo.

'What are you doing here?' she asked, trying to sound imperious.

'I saw you come here. Forgive me, Contessa, but I knew about the stairs and I was worried for you.'

The stairs. He mentioned the stairs particularly. Did he know of her past, had Luca told him that she had been almost insane and had tried to kill herself by throwing herself down the stairs? If he had she felt she would never forgive him. It was a lie and even if he believed it to be true, it was between them and not anyone else.

But of course, everyone that worked in the house had to know what had happened. The servants would be bound to gossip; it was probably a way of life to them. Yet it was maddening nonetheless.

However, in as calm a voice as possible she said. 'I cannot see why that would worry you.'

'When I first came and inspected this place, Contessa, there was no light bulb. I was not certain that someone had come and put a new one in. I thought you could have had an accident if you explored in the dark.'

'Believe me, Carlo, if there had been no light I would not have even crossed the room. I'm scared of rats!'

'There are rats but Antonio put down some poison. However, you can never be sure that they will take it.'

'God!' She looked up at him. 'Let's get out of here. Have you been down the cellar?'

'Yes, but not to the end. . . .'

'What do you mean – *not to the end*?'

'There is a narrow passageway. I am not sure where it leads. I wanted to explore myself but I hadn't a powerful torch. Do you want me to see where it leads?'

'No, that's not necessary; I can ask my husband when he comes back.'

They went back across the garden. They crossed to the loggia and when she came to the doors to the sunroom, she said she would go in there. Perhaps in the afternoon she would go out riding, she would let him know.

'Of course, Contessa. I am at your service.'

He bowed his head and departed silently. He was strange and yet he exuded something that gave her a little confidence in him. Perhaps it was that which made it important that he did not know of what she had previously been accused.

She rang for coffee and it was the happy smiling Claudia who came and brought it.

'Claudia, I was in the storerooms next to the indoor pool. There was a door and a flight of stairs that leads to a cellar, but there is a passage as well. Does that passage come into the house?'

Claudia laughed. 'Oh no, Contessa, it leads to the shore. You know the fort of course – you will come out there. You must have forgotten, Contessa, that the conte's ancestors were pirates and villains!'

Alva put a hand up over her mouth – of course, she recalled someone telling her that.

'So they used that for bringing in contraband of some kind?'

'*Sí*, Contessa. But many, many years ago, long before the conte was born! But in the war, the last war, of course, it was used sometimes by the partisans. But they were good, you understand, Contessa?'

'Yes, I'm sure they were. Thank you, Claudia, I had forgotten all about it.'

Claudia looked serious at once. 'But you will not go and use it, Contessa, it is dangerous. The conte said it must never be used as it is so dangerous. It could collapse, it is so old. He has forbidden everyone to go there.'

'Goodness, Claudia, I would never go down there. Heavens, I don't like confined spaces underground. I could never be a miner!'

'Good, but I know how adventurous the contessa is.'

'Not when it comes to dark passages that go underground, Claudia. I do promise you that.'

Later, she did go riding and requested that Carlo would accompany her. She was a little uneasy about going out alone and besides she knew that Carlo would attempt to follow her, and she preferred him where she could see him.

On the ride she told him about the cellar and the passageway and when they reached the shore, they raced their horses towards the tower.

'I remember being out here on my own. I saw the tower and the stairs that led down. It made me uneasy but I could not remember why. I still can't, but perhaps it was because I knew about its rather shady past. I am quite imaginative and perhaps I had pictured all kinds of evil deeds going on down there.'

'I should think it was just a way to store contraband, Contessa.'

'But you never know. Pirates were not the kindest of souls,' she smiled up at him.

'You could be right then. Still, it's good it makes you feel uneasy, that way you won't be tempted to go and explore the passageway.'

'Not now that Claudia has told me about it. And you shouldn't go down there either; she says it's not safe.'

'Very well, Contessa, I will not explore it. At least not until the conte is back.'

'I'll race you to the headland,' she said, turning her horse. It was wonderful and exhilarating to be out and free, galloping through the wavelets, feeling the wind on her face, its fingers tugging through her hair – it made her feel glad to be alive once more. It was this that she needed, this feeling of normality.

It was not a fair competition for Carlo let her win. Of course he would do so – she was, after all, the Contessa Mazareeze and he was her bodyguard. He could not know that to her a competition was a competition, no matter who was taking part. By the time they were riding side by side she felt too happy even to mention it. In fact her whole body glowed with a kind of unrestrained joy that made it completely unnecessary even to speak.

CHAPTER SEVEN

ROSA *d'Casta* – when the woman announced herself on the phone Alva pondered on what she could possibly want. She remembered the woman as being completely self-centred and practically ignoring Alva at the dinner party. Rosa had sent flowers to the hospital and Alva had written a note of thanks. She rather hoped that that had not been seen by Rosa as a gesture of wishing to strike up a friendship, but when Alva asked politely how Signora d'Casta was, the woman ignored the greeting and launched in, rather hysterically, with the statement that she had to see Alva.

'Believe me it is so important,' she emphasized.

'Well, what is it about?' Alva murmured, holding herself back a little.

'I cannot come there,' Rosa said, ignoring the question. 'You must come here to my villa, and you must come alone. Do not tell anyone that you are coming here!'

'I'm sorry. Signora but after what I have been through. . . .'

'If you think that is the end of it you are madder than I thought!'

Well, hardly an encouraging statement – Alva reeled slightly from it, feeling a film of perspiration break out on her upper lip.

'Listen to me! It is so important. I know that your husband

is away. I was very close to his wife, you know, we were friends . . . I know more than you can imagine and if you want me to help, you will come here and listen to me.'

'Why don't you come here?' Alva asked, recovering slightly. If anyone was deranged then she was certain it was the d'Casta woman.

'I cannot, walls have ears – isn't that what you English say? And believe me at the palazzo that is more so than anywhere. It is a place of secret passages and hidden doors.'

Well that was true, she supposed. Already Alva had discovered that there was a door behind a wonderfully carved panel in her room. Luca had shown it to her; he had said it was where one of his ancestors visited lady houseguests who had fallen under his spell.

'Charming!' she had said. 'I hope you never use it!'

'Well, I could use it to come to you . . . but its entrance is not in my bedroom. . . .'

'Thank goodness for that. If you ever ask me to change rooms when we have guests I warn you I will be terribly suspicious.'

Rosa's voice interrupted her reverie. 'Are you listening to me, Alva? I am not joking, I assure you, you are in danger, believe me I know plenty of things.'

'I don't understand?'

'About Luca and his first contessa. Renata's mother. Things are not what they seem. . . .'

'I don't really want to know,' Alva said, but a cold band had started to tighten inside her. She felt a shiver as if someone had walked over her grave. This was ridiculous – was the woman implying that Luca was not what *he* seemed. She remembered how Rosa d'Casta had been all over him at the dinner party. Hardly the actions of someone who loathed, or was afraid of the conte. Alva realized that the woman could be trying to cause trouble.

'I so want you to believe me, Alva! I know we did not get off to a good start but I do have your interest at heart. Remember the stairs, when you allegedly fell down, do you recall how you nearly died, Alva? Do you *believe* it was an accident?'

'I don't know what it was, but I do know that I never made a suicide attempt,' Alva said.

The woman had fired the right bullet: it met its target, Alva's desire to know the truth of what happened before she ended at the foot of the stairs. Curiosity vied with loyalty to Luca. Whatever had happened she could not believe that Luca had anything to do with it. There was no reason for Luca to do such a thing and, besides, instinct told her that Luca was a man to be trusted. However, the realization that she might learn something was too irresistible. She had to go.

'I don't know where you live? I can leave now but it might take me some time to shake off my bodyguard.'

'It is not hard to find my villa. As to your bodyguard, might I suggest that you. . . ?'

Lying did not come easily to Alva. Having to explain to Carlo that she had a headache and that she would spend the morning resting was a miserable experience. As it was, she avoided the man's eyes, busying herself in the kitchen, making a tray of tea things and brushing aside Claudia who wanted to do it for her. Yet everything had to be carefully done so that no one would suspect.

Once in her room she took from her wardrobe a black track suit, covering her silvery blonde hair with the hood of the jacket and feeling that it was all a little dramatic. However, Rosa d'Casta had assured her that she would not reveal anything unless Alva came alone.

Fortunately, she made the outside of the house without any problem. Crossing to the garage she met one of the stable boys but he knew nothing and merely acknowledged her. In the garage she mulled over which car to take and in the end took the small Fiat. It was a car that the servants often used to go into the village or down to the port. If anyone saw it gone they would assume someone had taken it and would hardly call a roll call of everyone on the estate to see who was missing.

Congratulating herself on her cunning, she drove slowly down the drive and beyond the gates. Once she reached the road that Rosa d'Casta had told her to take her confidence ebbed a little. It was a steep narrow road; the higher she climbed the narrower it appeared to be. On one side the land fell away down to the sea, the area covered with scrub, rather like the maquis in the south of France. On the other side there was a higher cliff, at the top a villa or two and then nothing.

Holding her foot to the brake she climbed slowly and carefully, hating the sound of rough stones breaking under the wheels.

As she turned a bend she almost skidded as she pulled up for a large brown dog. It was lying at the side of the road and for a moment she wondered if it had been hit by a car. Hesitantly, she unwound her window and called to it softly. It merely gazed at her with its huge soft brown eyes. The tinkle of bells sounded on the still air and she remembered the reason for the dog. Around the bend came two men with a herd of goats, the coats of the animals long and glossy, their expression haughty, as they were herded down the road. That was what the goat herders did; they sent the dog ahead to warn oncoming traffic that the animals were being brought down from the high hills.

The men touched their caps as they passed by the side of her car and one murmured. '*Buon giorno*, Contessa.' She nodded and smiled, she had not wanted to be seen but the two men were hardly likely to rush to a telephone and tell the people back at the palazzo that the contessa was driving somewhere alone. The island had its own ways, her husband was their employer but islanders did not know everything that went on.

Thankfully, she came to the last turn and the road evened out. High on a promontory at the very peak was the pink villa that Rosa d'Casta leased. Alva recalled that Luca had told her it had been Rosa's home for many years but no matter how close she had become to Luca and his first wife, she had not been allowed to purchase the villa. Besides, she had a house that she owned in Florence and to where she usually went in the winter. However, this time she had stayed for longer than usual.

The gates were thrown back. Alva drove through, deciding to park right outside the front door. There was no other car around so there had to be a garage. The front door was open, but between that and the entrance hallways was a glass door that was firmly closed.

Alva saw a bell pull on the stonework by the open door and pulled on that. Its clanging sound echoed back to her. Stepping into the small vestibule she went up to the glass door. There was no pattern on the glass and so she peered through, but the hallway was rather dark. There was no light filtering in from a window. Stepping back she rang the bell again and wondered whether Rosa had servants or not.

Thinking the woman might be at the back of the house, or perhaps in the garden, she wandered along the front of the house. There were windows, but they were shuttered, she could see no gate or entrance that would lead her to the back. There was just a high stone wall at the end of the house. Puzzled she went back to the front door, stepped inside and after ringing the bell waited once more.

When no one came she pushed the glass door, it swung open. Apprehensively, she stepped into the hall; there was a sweet smell of jasmine but it was artificial as if it came from a scent spray or furniture polish.

Gingerly she moved through the house, calling out 'Rosa?' as she went. There was no sound. Directly in front of her there was a heavy wooden door – it was very dark in the hallway and she thought she would have had to have a window put in somewhere to let in light, but then conceded that perhaps it was beautiful and cool on steamy summer days.

Opening the door partly, she peered around. It led into a sitting-room. Again it was rather dim as the shutters at the windows were closed.

The tiled floor echoed her footsteps back to her. It was a huge room, beautifully furnished with a chaise longue and sofas covered in pale blue silk. As she moved across the room the sole of her shoe felt as if it were attaching itself to a gluey substance. She looked down. Something had spilled on the floor but she could not make it out . . . was it wine? But no, it was too thick. 'Rosa,' Alva called, rushing across the room. Her feet encountered a pale rug in front of the shutters. Quickly, her fingers trembling, she unhooked the bolt on the shutters and flung them back. Vivid light spilled into the room, highlighting the substance she had trailed through. Across the carpet there were bright red footprints; mesmerized, she stared at them for a long moment. Her heart started to thud against her chest and, placing a hand there, she pressed hard as if this would still the rapid beat.

The substance she had walked through was scarlet, it trailed across the room . . . it spattered across a pale wood occasional table, to the right of the table was a bundle, like a pile of rags.

Crossing the carpet in the direction of the heap of rags, her feet slid on to the tiled surface once more and she almost skidded. Bending down she put her fingers into the substance and then quickly jerked upwards. Her finger tips were covered in the liquid, only it was not liquid as such, rubbing the tip of her thumb over the red stuff, she at once recognized it as blood. A little gasp escaped from her; turning again, she stared at the rags, or what she had thought were rags. Going closer, she saw it was a shawl of vivid reds and blues and it covered the head and shoulders of a body. Pale fawn trousers were on the lower half of the body and spots of blood were there too.

Her body shaking now, she bent, pulling at the shawl, it slid away easily enough . . . there was dark hair spread out over the floor. The back of the head looked like squashed, soft fruit. There was pulp and something greyish spilling out . . . tiny fragments of pale pith, that later she would realize were bone.

Realization was slow to come and she just stared at the battered head of Rosa d'Casta and then she gagged, dropped the shawl and turned away, only seconds later to turn back to put her bloodstained fingers to the woman's neck. Rosa's flesh was still slightly warm but there was no pulse. The woman was dead.

Fearful for her own safety, Alva backed away, stumbling out of the room and out into the hall, only to stop and lean against one of the wooden panels in the dim hallway. She listened. There was absolute silence apart from the loud thud of her own racing heart.

Police – ambulance – her head was empty of numbers: she could not think what the emergency number was. An image of the woman's head flashed before her eyes; she felt bile rise up in her throat and, as well, a terrible pity moved through her. Quickly, she shook the vivid picture out of her mind, heading determinedly for the door. Once outside she sought for breath, for calm, and went and got into her car, careful to lock all the doors.

On the seat next to her was her mobile phone. She might

not remember the number of the emergency service but she knew by heart the number of the palazzo. Carlo would know what to do. . . .

Before she finished putting in the number there was the sound of a car – a siren. Looking in the mirror she saw the familiar shape of a police car drive too quickly through the gate, only to brake as the driver saw the Fiat. The squeal of brakes was deafening but he somehow managed to turn the wheel and collide not with her but with a cluster of terracotta plant pots that shattered on impact.

Before she could get out of the car they were on to her, guns in hand, trying to open the car door, ordering her to get out, not to try anything.

Timidly she unlocked the door; before she could open it one of the policemen dragged it open. She held her hands, palms up, as if to say calm down but the policeman took no notice and dragged her unceremoniously from the car, turning her around and patting her down roughly.

She wanted to say, 'How dare you?', but she knew that would antagonize them so she merely acquiesced without saying anything.

The other policeman suddenly seemed to recognize her. He said in rapid Italian. '*Dio Mio*, it is the contessa.'

'*E allora*!'

The man searching her body with more enthusiasm than necessity suddenly let her go. Turning around she glanced at the police car. There was someone huddled in the back.

'Show me your hands!' the policeman now demanded. Palms turned up she revealed the damning evidence of blood.

'Someone has done something terrible to Signora d'Casta,' she said. 'In the sitting-room, please go and see, I don't think she's alive but I can't be certain.'

'Go and look,' the policeman said to the man who had searched her, 'I'll stay out here.'

Alva stood now with arms folded at her waist, leaning back against the car. Her body burned with the humiliation of the man's rough and intimate search. She felt dirty. *It is nothing,* her conscience told her, *think about what has happened to Rosa d'Casta.*

Now the door to the police car opened a little. A tiny woman emerged, thin and pale with fright, not too young but not old. 'Sir, I did not see this lady. . . .'

'Zitto! Get back in the car!'

'Officer, you surely do not think that I had anything to do with this,' Alva said. 'I found the *signora,* I was about to call you. . . .'

He said nothing, not making eye contact. The other policeman came out. 'She's dead, skull bashed in,' he glanced at her. 'Sort of thing a woman would do, you know, one turns away, the other bitch decides she's had enough, boom, bang. . . .'

'Any weapon?'

'Nothing that I can see, better call the chief . . . we need forensics.'

'Contessa, you will have to come with us, the commissario will require you to make a statement.'

'Of course,' she agreed.

'You do know that will be on the mainland?'

'No, I didn't know that. I want to co-operate but I must insist I come in later. When my husband is here, I have not been well and. . . .'

The men exchanged a look, debating the point with their eyes. She knew they were wondering how tough they should be. Mentally questioning how far they dare go with her.

'You have to know that my life was threatened too. . . .'

'We heard something,' the one she decided to describe as arrogant muttered.

'Call the commissario now,' she demanded, coming out of her shock and fear. After all, she was innocent and would not be pushed around by these two, one who was obviously relishing humiliating her, and probably for some political purpose.

'Perhaps you could give us a statement now,' the marginally milder of the two suggested.

'Let me call it in first,' the other said.

As he went to the car, the sudden spurt of confidence had weakened Alva and her legs started to tremble. 'Perhaps I could sit down,' she murmured, then when no answer came, opened the door of her car and slid on to the seat. Her phone was there, she picked it up, looked at the policeman and quirked an eyebrow in an unspoken question. He nodded, probably thinking she was going to call some hotshot lawyer.

Luca's telephone number was at the top of her list of stored numbers. She highlighted and pressed 'call'. It was answered in seconds.

'*Cara*,' he murmured, full of warmth and pleasure, as if the call were important and welcome to him. 'I was going to call you, I am at the port and I will—'

'Luca, something terrible has happened. . . .'

Luca was obviously speaking to someone high up in police society. 'If it were my ancestors they would have cut off his balls and made him eat them.'

'Luca!' Alva whispered, horrified.

'How dare he pat down my wife so intimately? There is no need for that machismo from that *coglione*. The contessa was distraught, she found Rosa d'Casta with her head smashed in . . . she was in shock. Who are these men masquerading as cops you have sent me? I want replacements.'

Obviously, soothing words were being said on the other end of the line. She watched as Luca, hand tightened around the telephone receiver, marched around his desk, back ramrod straight, head thrown back, anger making him pale.

'I know,' he said at last, the words almost a sigh. 'But have you ever seen my wife . . . she is a tiny thing, I doubt she could hit anything hard enough. . . .'

'Oh yes I could, if I needed too,' she murmured. He turned; obviously he heard her for he winked.

The telephone call came to an end and he put the phone in its cradle and turned to face her, leaning his hip against the desk. She was sitting in a chair in front of him. How quickly he had come home to her, dropping everything, arriving in hours. Caring for her so tenderly, she wondered how she had ever wanted to leave him.

'Oh Luca,' she went to him, pleased when he drew her close, wrapping her in his arms. Only then did she feel truly safe. 'What is happening, Luca? What is going on in this idyllic world of yours?'

'I wish I knew, *cara*, but I don't. When I think of what could have happened to you. Promise me you will never do anything like that again?'

'I won't. I think I have learned my lesson the hard way, but Rosa was so convincing, she told me she knew something about . . . about—' But she stopped, how she could tell him that what Rosa had told her hinted that he knew something about her fall down the stairs. It would surely wrench them apart again if he thought that she suspected him of involvement. Quickly she sought around for something to say.

'I don't care what gossip she had for you. Gossip is not important. Besides, Rosa was a woman who imagined she was in love with me. She would only want to make mischief; she could say nothing important about anything.' he said.

Ah, he had not realized it was something serious to do with him. That above all proved his innocence to her; if he had done something wrong he would be questioning her more closely to find out if she knew anything.

'The commissario will come here. He's on his way; he will

talk to you but I am going to be here all the time – you just have to tell the truth.'

But what was the truth? What could she say about what Rosa had said to her? If she told him exactly verbatim would that not pour suspicion on Luca? After all, the woman had hinted at something about Luca and his first wife. She knew she was a bad liar – the words needed to put an end to this terrible matter would not come easily to her, yet she had to try.

'Luca, you are home early, I didn't expect you until tomorrow?'

'My business was over and I decided not to go and see Renata. As well, really, she will be home the moment she hears about Rosa. They were very close. She will be devastated.'

Alva's heart sank. On top of everything else she must contend with the sulky and resentful Renata – but at the same time she knew there was nothing she could do about it. There was no way that she could show that she did not want the girl to come to her own home, no matter how unpleasant Renata would make life.

'Are you sure, Alva, there is nothing else that Rosa said?' Luca asked the question nonchalantly. He was standing at the window, partly turned away from her.

If she loved him as she knew she did, then why hold back the truth. Show that Rosa had meant to cause trouble between them perhaps. Damn her memory, if she was cognizant of the past then she knew there was nothing she could not share with him. But it was this lack of memory that made her hesitate. How did she know? She could not even remember what Luca had said about his first wife in the past. Of course he had recently told her that Silvia had died in a road traffic accident. That Renata had been with her. He had said they were on their way home from Rosa's villa. Yet there was nothing sinister in any of that . . . speak up, her mind urged, but something tugged the thought back. Forget it. It has nothing to do with anything. He was probably right about Rosa; she had wanted him and wanted to make trouble to make her go away. That was all it was, a woman in love with a man who did not want her.

The commissario when he arrived was about forty, dressed in a suit that was most definitely not off the peg, his grooming highly polished. He had a hard, intelligent face and an overly large nose. He was small and wiry but exuding confidence. His politeness, she suspected was a veneer. Obviously, he was one ruthless cop and Luca had told her that he had risen up from the ranks. A Roman, he had transferred to the coastal fringe at his own request.

'I suspect,' Luca told her, 'that he was spawned in the slums and knew intimately too many villains. Here he is an unknown quantity and can be what he wants. He is not so bad, as cops go.'

Alva could see where Luca got his assessment. The man had the stamp of someone who had had to pull himself up out of the streets but she did not find him in the least intimidating. Again, she suspected it was because of her ability to mix with so many different kinds of people. Probably it was why she had been good at her job in the past, that – more than ability with a word processor and telephone – had made her indispensable to Tony. Again the confirming thought just popped into her mind and she accepted it.

'So, Contessa, perhaps you would tell me what happened? If you do not mind, from the beginning. I believe Signora d'Casta telephoned you and asked you to visit her, is that right?'

Taking a deep breath, Alva held it inside her for a few moments. She allowed herself to look directly at the commissario; his dark eyes were hard and his expression like that of a hawk examining its prey. He was not going to let her intimidate him, he had obviously decided, no matter her position. All the deference he had shown when he had first come in had gone; now he was professional. All men were created equal in his eyes – that would be his mantra. Alva knew the type and there would be just the tiniest core of resentment at the conte's position, as if the commissario suspected that the conte imagined he could buy himself out of trouble with any authority. If only he knew, Alva thought, the opposite was true of Luca. He was not a man like that – or, Alva was certain, she could not love him.

'*Cara*,' Luca urged as if he suspected she had slipped into a trance, which in effect, she realized she had.

'I'm sorry, Commissario. You must know that I lost my memory; things come hard for me.'

'You cannot remember daily happenings?'

'Oh no, I did not mean that. Thank God, I haven't any sign of dementia. No, it is just that when I am going about my business things slip in and out of my head. Things that are not connected with what I'm doing. A memory, well a fraction of a memory to be exact, I had that just now. Something about my husband' – she turned and smiled at Luca – 'a rather pleasant realization about him.'

Luca looked back at her, unsure whether to smile or not.

'But, I must get to the business at hand. Poor Rosa. Yes, she called. She was a little hysterical—'

'What do you mean?' The hawk pinned her down.

'Well, she said she had to see me but would not tell me what it was about. She was rather mysterious about it,' which, Alva thought, was not entirely a lie. 'And she couldn't come here, I had to go there and I had to go alone. It was all rather strange because the *signora* and I were not close friends. I mean I don't even know if I met her more than once?' She looked at Luca.

'You did, but not very much. I think if you met her at three social occasions that was it,' he explained. 'My wife met Signora d'Casta again at a dinner party a couple of weeks ago, here at the palazzo. For myself I cannot imagine why she wanted to see the contessa, unless . . . do you think she might have some information about the man that took you away, Alva. Did she say anything about that?'

'Not a thing. As I said, she would not tell me anything over the telephone.'

'Well go on, Contessa, you agreed to go and you left the house without telling anyone.'

Alva went on to explain about Carlo. How he was her bodyguard but Signora d'Casta had insisted she go alone, and so she had deceived the staff and Carlo into thinking she was going to lie down.

'Why not tell them the truth?'

'I thought that Carlo might follow me. He would believe that my husband would expect that of him. I admit, I'm a curious cat and if anyone tells me they want to reveal something I have to go for it. Inquisitive mind, I suppose. Besides, I thought she might be ill or something. She sounded so strange. With hindsight I realize it was silly of me. I should've had Carlo follow me – hindsight is great but it isn't walking by your side when you make these stupid decisions.'

'Yes, I can appreciate that. So you arrived at the villa and you saw no one and no one passed you on the road.'

'No one, well there were just a couple of goatherds and their dog, but no one in a car or walking. Goodness, had I met a car I'm sure I would have died – how would they get past?'

'There are passing places,' the commissario said with serious concern, as if he doubted her ability to be a safe driver. 'So then you arrived, what happened then?'

This took longer, as she began to explain how she had gone into the drawing-room and opened the shutters, the horror revisited her. She started to shiver and Luca crossed the room to sit next to her, wrapping a comforting arm around her.

'The contessa is cold; perhaps a wrap would be good for her?' suggested the commisario.

He obviously thought he was being crafty, but Luca was on to him. There was no way he would leave her alone. Going to the telephone he buzzed for a servant and asked for a wrap for the contessa.

It was accomplished in moments; the youngest maid had been dispatched to run up to the contessa's bedroom and to come back with a shawl. The shawl was thick cashmere, a single green colour but it still reminded Alva of the shawl that had covered Rosa d'Casta's head, the terrible scene that she had witnessed as she had removed the shawl.

'Perhaps we could have some tea,' Alva murmured to no one in particular but the maid obviously took it on herself to go and order it.

It was Claudia who brought it in. They had sat in silence as Alva had merely stared at the carpet unable to bring herself to relive those horrid moments.

'I'm sorry,' she said not for the first time. 'I can't do it . . . give me a moment.'

'Take as long as you like. It is important that what you say is accurate,' the commissario said.

'Take some tea,' Luca urged, pouring some into the thin white china cup.

Her hand trembled as she reached for the cup; folding the offending hand in the other she rubbed it, as if this would end the tremor. Oddly, it worked. She took up the cup and sipped the pale brown liquid.

'You must think I am an idiot,' she said to the commissario.

'He thinks no such thing, Alva; you have been through so much. People understand that.'

'Tell me, Conte, do you think the two could be connected.

What happened to the contessa and what happened to Rosa d'Casta?'

Silence hung in the room; it was there even in the tiny dust motes that floated in a beam of sunlight.

'I don't see how it can,' Luca said. 'They have no connection. They were not friends; they shared no mutual secrets, or did you, *cara*?' He turned and looked at her kindly.

'No, of course we didn't. I couldn't stand the woman.'

There was a gasp from somewhere, maybe herself or Luca or perhaps the commissario. She realized when the words popped out that she could practically be condemning herself.

'No,' she said, 'I've said it; I won't try to explain it because I can't. I met her for what I thought was the first time at the dinner party. She came late with some feeble excuse; she monopolized my husband all evening and was rude to everyone else. But for doing that I would not invite her again. I don't think it warranted my going to her home and battering her over the head with some terrible instrument.'

'You were jealous of her?'

'Of course she was not, what is she to be jealous of?' Luca snapped.

'No, not jealous exactly, I was annoyed with her. But I think I am rather used to women trying to steal my husband from me. I think it happened a lot. It did, didn't it?' she shot a look at Luca.

He shrugged. 'I don't know really . . . but perhaps. . . .'

She warmed to his modesty; he did not want to admit that women found him irresistible. . . . Ping, there it was – another little dart letting light into her dark mind.

'Anyway, this isn't relevant,' she put her cup back on the saucer. 'Now . . . now I think I can tell you what I found when I went into the drawing-room.' Tugging the cashmere shawl close around her, she started her description and did not stop until she told him about running from the house and of sitting in the car and not being able to remember the emergency number.

'Then, when I started to ring the palazzo, the police arrived. I don't know how they knew what had happened. . . .'

But the commissario was not going to reveal that, he ignored the statement saying.

'No one was at the villa; there was no car, there was nothing?'

'No one was there, there wasn't a car, at least I didn't see one.'

He sighed.

'You see how difficult it is conte. The Contessa passed no one on the road, apart from the *paesano*, the police coming the other way also say they passed no one and yet someone had been and killed the *signora*.'

'But they could have escaped before the police set off.'

'The police were in the area. They had been to visit someone over a traffic accident. When the servant, Maria, heard the screams she ran away. To the villa that is just beyond the *signora*'s home. They telephoned and the police were there in seconds, as the contessa has confessed.'

'I can see it looks strange,' Alva said, trying to sound calm and reasonable but her heart had started to go like an express train. It looked as if she could be accused of what she had not done. The evidence was certainly not fanciful.

'But the girl . . . Maria, I think you said . . . when she saw me she left the car and said something . . . the policeman was very rude to her but she pointed to me and said . . . what?'

'That the person was a man. She had caught a glimpse of trousers, but you were wearing trousers.'

'But she did not see my wife's car!'

'She saw no car but as you know, Conte, since you own the property, that there are huge bushes across the courtyard where people often parked because it offers shade. A small car would not be noticed there. The contessa could have put her car there and then have been driving away just as the police arrived.'

'I was facing the wrong direction. My rear was to the police car, I had not turned around as I would have done if I were coming from the bushes.'

The commissario was staring at her now. She had not missed the sarcasm when he had said that *'since you own the property,'* to the conte, as if that implied that perhaps Rosa d'Casta was allowed to live there because she was more than a friend.

It could be true, Alva thought, the woman could have been his mistress. After all, they had been separated some time and he was a man who— Wildly, she looked at him, was that it? Was that why the commissario was suspicious of her – because the murdered woman and Luca had been lovers? In a place like Santa Caterina things were never kept secret for long, she knew that only too well.

'There is that – you were only sitting in the car, you had not started the engine and you were not where you should have been had you wanted to hide yourself. Unfortunately, contessa, your fingerprints are the only other ones in the room, you touched the body, and you had blood on your hands. . . .'

'It came off the shawl when I lifted it and I touched Rosa's neck to find a pulse.'

'This is ridiculous!' Luca exploded. 'Do you really imagine my wife could do that? Look at her, she is so frail. . . .'

'One blow could have felled the woman and then while she was down she could have been beaten senseless.'

'*Could* have been,' Luca picked up on the 'could' that seemed to add doubt to this theory.

'Our experts believe that is what happened. The *signora*

was struck, she fell to the floor and then continued to be beaten. We know this because she had put up her hands and they were covered with bruises. . . .'

'Oh my God,' Alva gasped. 'That is so—' She started to shake again, her imagination illuminating the scene in her mind. She put up her hands behind her head as if it were she who was warding off the terrible blows. 'That poor woman, what could she have known, or done to make someone hate her like that?'

'Hate? Yes, it did look as if someone really hated her. *A woman's kind of hatred.*'

Alva looked at the commissario feeling helpless. A wave of tiredness hit her, her eyelids fluttered, if she let herself she could drift away. Was this why she had been saved from the sea, just so that she could now be accused of murdering someone? Better to have drowned, or for her to have died when the car tried to run her down, or even when she had allegedly *fallen* down the stairs. The brief bout of happiness she had clawed back was now eroding fast. It was as if someone with a motive wanted to punish her . . . but for what?

'No weapon has been found,' the commissario murmured. 'And you Contessa would have had no time to hide it somewhere where it would not be found. I do not think it was you. I might be overruled when the evidence is examined once more, but I doubt it. You have no real motive, if you did not like the woman, well then I do not like many people but I would not beat them to death. And as the conte has consistently pointed out, you have been a victim yourself. I believe it is a conspiracy but how and why I do not know. However, I do assure you I will find out.'

If only that were the end of it, Alva thought, in the wake of the commissario's departure. But it was not to be. A deal had had to be struck, or an arrangement made, as the Commissario put it.

Luca held her close to him, they were sitting on the sofa and the afternoon sun had fled the sky. Neither had bothered to light lamps, preferring the dim glow of late afternoon.

'I don't like it,' Luca said, not for the first time.

'I don't like it much either, Luca, but if it brings the rats from their nests then I am all for it. Do you think it could all be connected as he suspects, that somehow Rosa and I shared a secret?'

'I wish I knew for certain but I really doubt it. You had nothing in common with Rosa. I think it a coincidence.'

The commissario had asked them both not to say anything about Alva's ordeal, not to let anyone know that as far as he was concerned he believed her story. The less said about it the better it would be. He would talk with the magistrate, of course, but if the real killer thought he was in the clear, he might yet overplay his hand. If suspicion still rested on the contessa he might even try to speak with her to find out just what she knew.

'But you must be careful. You must never go anywhere without protection,' the commissario told her. 'No matter who calls or whatever they tell you. You could be in real danger, Contessa.'

'I think I am in danger whatever,' she had said. And when she had said the words she was amazed how less afraid she felt. There was nothing she could do about it, but she could protect herself. She would not go out without Luca or Carlo. No one would tempt her again, no matter what they said they had to tell her. Fear had put her on the alert; it had sharpened her senses. She would be strong and she would use the adrenalin pumping through her to good advantage.

'Someone believes I know something and Rosa knew something too. But the two might not be connected. You know, I rather gave the impression to Antonio that I was well again, that I remembered things. . . .'

'Antonio? But why should what you told him matter?'

Ah, he liked Antonio and trusted him. After all, he was the one who had lied about her throwing herself down the stairs, but he was the one that Luca had believed instead of her.

'Perhaps he said something to someone else or it was repeated elsewhere and whoever wanted to harm me heard it and panicked.'

'It seems unlikely,' Luca said softly. 'Besides, Antonio is not a gossip. No, it does not come from here. It is someone, somewhere, who does not care whether you have remembered or not. They are just afraid that you might remember.'

'All right,' she whispered, letting him believe what he wished. Anyway, Luca could be right. If she carried a secret then she was a danger while she lived because if she regained her memory she could expose them. Better that they did not take the risk of her memory returning. They could not wait for that to happen, they had to act before it did.

'It's cold,' she said, snuggling against him.

'I think it is time we lighted the fire would you like that? A real fire . . . come here,' he held her to him tightly. 'My poor brave, Alva, you should not have to go through all this.'

'I know, I should just live a normal life, but it seems I'm not destined for that. And yes, Luca, I should love a real fire . . . and a glass of wine before dinner . . . I want to chase it all out of me, Luca and just enjoy this night. . . .'

'Then that is what you will do, let me call for Guido. . . .'

CHAPTER EIGHT

ALVA had vivid dreams. She awakened slowly, as if not wanting the reality to intrude. Luca lay on his side beside her. He was sleeping, his face worry free, and looking younger in repose, the concerns and worries he had for her obliterated by deep sleep. Her dreams had gone further back than her time with Luca. She had dreamed of her parents. For the first time since she had been run over, she saw their faces. Her mother was like her, blonde and small and delicate, her physical attributes hiding the toughness inside her, her dad was taller, darker, with friendly blue eyes.

They were always busy – kind and friendly but not particularly doting. They wanted to save the world; their interests and ideals meant she had to share their love with all the things they passionately cared about. She was lonely as a little girl, and then when she went to school she had had to fend for herself. She had been seven at the time. There she found love with Chloe and it was to Chloe's home that she went when her parents were abroad at Christmas and Easter.

Chloe's parents were conventional parents and they had been so good to her. When Chloe died they retreated into themselves and she remembered them telling her, on one of her visits, not to come and see them again. She reminded them too much of Chloe and the happy times. It hurt so much when Chloe died that it was better they did not see Alva. It broke her heart a second time but she respected their wishes, only later learning that they had gone abroad to live, to try to make a new life. Now, remembering those happy times when she was a child, she hoped that they had found something to salvage from their broken lives.

Lying back against the pillow, she closed her eyes, going over so many small treasured memories that seemed to shoot through her mind. There were little explosions of light, her mind was a shooting star . . . Aunt Beatrice, hateful woman, so cold and resentful of having to look after the child her sister and her husband had orphaned.

She could have refused but there was the money. Her parents had insurance and a house that was sold at the right time when property values were racing away. Had Aunt Beatrice had control of the estate? When Alva came into her majority perhaps there was very little left. Luca seemed to have hinted at some time that her aunt had charge of her finances. Perhaps any money had been spent – after all, her school was expensive; she never missed a school trip and if she wished to go away with Chloe and her parents, Aunt Beatrice had never refused. There was money to keep her while she was at university. She seemed to recall her aunt saying there would be enough for her to buy a small property of her own. Yet she did not remember if she had bought a house, or what had happened to the proceeds of any sale.

Luca stirred, his eyes opened slowly; turning, he propped himself up on his elbow gazing up at her. 'You look flushed, Alva, are you all right?'

'Yes and no, I had vivid dreams last night.'

The words spilled out of her, explaining what the dreams had caused her to remember. He sat up and hugged her to him, running a hand through her hair.

'I wanted to tell you but I did not think it right. You told me all this – about that dreadful woman. There was money, Alva, but we could not get our hands on it, although we tried.'

'So she stole from me?'

'Appropriated perhaps is the word. I think she enjoyed herself but it would be difficult to prove. It would have meant lawyers and court cases and you did not think it worthwhile.'

'All right,' she sighed. 'But that is not what someone tried to kill me for was it?'

'No.' His hand tightened on her soft blonde hair, its silvery colour shining out against the brown of his skin, and he threaded her hair through his fingers, as if it were skeins of silk. 'The idea of your aunt hiring a hit man is a rather bizarre image. I want to laugh at it as a ludicrous idea, but it isn't funny, *cara*.'

'Oh, but it is. I know what you mean. Now that I can see her, small and thin, without my mother's prettiness. The older sister, resentful of the younger one. I don't think it was me she hated, but my mother. No, I don't think she would harm me in a physical way and, as you say, she wouldn't know how.'

They lay in silence for long moments; beneath her ear she could hear the steady beat of his heart. Luca . . . it came again that feeling of overwhelming love that had moved her years ago. She stayed where she was, still enjoying the feeling, bathing in the luscious feelings down deep inside her. Head over heels, that was what it was. After that first meeting when he had rubbed her up the wrong way, the second had been more electrifying. She remembered it as if it had always been there, as if she had never forgotten him.

He called to ask her out. At first she prevaricated, only changing her mind when it seemed he was going to give up. They drove out in the country somewhere, a small inn, away from the political crowd. A mind-numbing shyness had come over her; she could not eat, could not talk, only able to respond to what he was saying with monosyllabic words.

'What is it, Alva? Am I boring you?' he had asked at last, slightly exasperated by her inability to be herself.

'On the contrary,' she had said.

'I am sorry, I do not understand?'

She had babbled then, going on about a book she had read where the heroine said. 'I can't breathe quite right when I'm with you.'

'*The Last Tycoon*,' he said. 'F Scott Fitzgerald's wonderful but unfinished novel.'

'Gosh, how did you know that?'

'You think I wouldn't because I am an Italian?'

'No, it's just that you don't look like the type of man who would read books.'

How he had laughed. He had thought that really funny. 'I do it all the time,' he confessed, 'with all the travelling I do, long plane trips, lonely hotel rooms. . . .'

He took up her hand that was resting on the table, holding it lightly in his own. 'And perhaps I could say the same thing, only . . . perhaps it is the opposite . . . I breathe too much when I am with you.'

Luca, she thought, again. How did you come to fall in love with me? I was so stupid. But she did not ask. Dare not, knowing that Luca when he had a mind, could be brutal with the truth and she was afraid of what the answer might be.

'Let us go riding today,' he said. 'It is a perfect winter morning.'

'How do you know, the shutters are closed?'

'I feel it in my bones.' He left her then, gently parting from her, going across the room and opening the shutters. Sure enough, thin winter sunshine drizzled itself into the room.

'There, I knew I was right.'

'Then we will.' She lay back and stretched. 'But after coffee and rolls . . . mm, Luca . . . everything is going pear-shaped but I feel so happy today . . . is that wrong?'

'Of course it isn't wrong. You deserve that feeling of happiness, Alva, so enjoy it.'

She had a flash of memory, it was just after Renata had arrived and it was momentous.

Renata chased away her happiness. Her arrival came with a fierce squall that had windows and doors rattling. Trees were bent backwards, and plant pots fell over. A winter storm, Luca said, and it could last for days.

Renata was not impolite but cold – or rather, cool, Alva amended. She spoke when spoken to by Alva but did not initiate conversation herself. They met mostly at mealtimes, at least the girl came to table and although she picked at her food, she was not rude.

She missed being beautiful. Alva noted that about her: attractive, striking certainly, with that thick dark hair, albeit brutally styled, and flashing dark eyes, but her features were very strong; her nose dominant in a small, high-cheekboned face. Her lips were thin too, although the lower had a curve that showed that somewhere inside her there was warmth and humour.

She dressed beautifully, having a sense of style that belied her nineteen years. Modern but classic was her style but she could certainly put things together and wore clothes well.

Coming across her in the sitting-room, Alva said, 'It was kind of you to send me the fruit, Renata. I did appreciate it.'

Renata looked up, her lips forming a little pout as if she were mulling over something.

'It wasn't my idea. My father told me to do it.'

'I see. Well, he shouldn't have forced you to do that, but it was kind of you to take the trouble to do as he asked. You could have refused.'

'I could have,' she said.

Alva smiled a little.

'What's funny?' Renata demanded.

'I was thinking that you are a lot like your father. I think that *he* finds it impossible to lie as well.'

'You think so?' Renata shrugged. 'But I do speak my mind,' she added.

Instead of retreating, as she did when coming across Renata anywhere, Alva went and sat in the easy chair. Guido had been to light the fire and it roared in the grate. The day was dull and although it was only three o'clock it was turning dark outside.

'Did you . . . were you very friendly with Rosa d'Casta?' Alva asked. Only that day at lunch had she heard Renata asking her father if there would be a funeral and where and when it would be. He had told her in Firenze – Florence – she had left a request in her will to be buried with her family.

Renata was a long time answering. As the seconds ticked away to minutes, Alva thought that perhaps she had pushed too hard. That Renata was not yet ready to have a conversation with her. That the frigid politeness should have given her the clue that Renata would never be friendly towards her, nor accept her marriage to her father.

At last she did speak and her words caused an implosion inside Alva.

'I hated the bitch.'

Alva tried not to gasp but failed.

'Shocked? Well you shouldn't be shocked, Alva, you know how I hated you. I can hate with a passion, you know.'

'I don't know how you hated me, Renata, I don't remember.'

'That's good, if you ask me. If you did remember then you would not be sitting there calmly talking to me.'

'Perhaps not,' Alva admitted. 'I'm not a saint.'

'No, you're not,' the girl admitted quietly. 'But she was a

whore,' Renata went on in a reasonable voice. 'A pimping little whore. She and my mother . . . they were the best of friends. Oh, everyone thought that – but I knew what happened at the villa and in Firenze.'

Alva stared at the girl. Renata left her seat and came to stand over Alva. 'Are you shocked? You've gone very pale, Alva. They both were, Silvia and Rosa, whores. You know why my mother was always there – up at the villa? To meet her lovers! She thought I didn't know, that I thought she was working. Oh, she was working all right but it had nothing to do with her art!'

'Renata I don't think you should—'

'Tell you? Why not? Didn't my father ever tell you about *her*, his first contessa? How she had all these men, she and Rosa. Oh, so classy on the outside but such bitches on the inside. I hated her for what she did to my father. The humiliation she poured on his head!'

As she stood, Alva watched, transfixed, and she saw the girl crumble before her eyes, the little body folding into itself, the great wracking sobs that came from her. There were no tears; it was too late for Renata to shed any tears – all Renata could do was let out these great wracking sobs.

Alva left her seat, gathering the girl to her. At first she struggled from the embrace and then she settled, as if Alva's soothing voice had a calming affect.

'It was not your fault, Renata, you must not blame yourself . . . you were a child . . . you could not have done anything. . . .'

'I thought you would be the same . . . that you would find other men, that you had found other men. . . .'

'Renata, how could I have found other men with that big lump on my tummy? But I understand – oh, Renata you have no idea how much I understand.'

They sat in the dimming light, finding some kind of

comfort in the flickering firelight. Renata let everything out; it was as if once she started she could not stop. The humiliation of being used by her mother, for Silvia had used her daughter. If Luca thought she was out with her daughter then she would not be up to her usual carrying-on.

'He did not care what she did in Firenze, but she brought it here, to the island. He did not want that . . . I knew that but I thought he would not believe me. And I was torn, not knowing who to turn to. Should I betray my mother, would they both never forgive me? I was so confused.'

'Renata, you were twelve years old, you should never have had to carry that burden. It was too much.'

'It was a relief when she died but I felt . . . I felt so guilty. I was quarrelling with her, you know what that road is like, if I had not been arguing with her she might still be alive. It was my fault she died.'

'You must not believe that, Renata. It happened, it was an accident, and it was not *your* fault. If you were arguing then your mother should have stopped the car.'

'She hit me, turned away from the road and slapped me hard and then we were going down, the car turning around and around, bumping, crashing . . . *I can still hear her screaming.*'

'Oh, Renata, Renata, if only you had told me this before . . . you should not have carried it all this time. . . .' Alva held on to her once more, soothing her, running her hands through the dark hair.

'I couldn't tell him. If I told him the truth I would have to tell him what she had been doing. I couldn't do that!'

'I understand, but Renata you need to when you are stronger. And you need to talk to someone professional who will make it go away for you.'

Renata looked up at Alva, studying her, showing that she was wondering if she had done the right thing. Alva knew the girl had to be feeling vulnerable and somehow Alva had pressed a button that had made her release it all.

'I've been doing stupid things,' Renata said, and then she unbuttoned the cuff on her stylish shirt and showed the cuts up her arm.

'Oh, Renata, my darling ... you have punished yourself enough without this. How long has this been going on?'

'A few months. I'm a freak at university, no one has these feelings inside them, and no one's been through it all. I don't think I can stay there; I can't get on with anyone. And now ... now is not the time, what with what has happened but I can't go on ... I'm sorry, Alva, but I can't.'

Thoughts flashed through Alva's mind. She remembered someone else who had had this problem. A girl at school, she cut herself and one day went too far and was rushed to hospital. She never returned to school. Renata's mental state was as bad if not worse. She did not suffer only from a low opinion of herself, nor did she want to seize attention, but she wanted to punish herself.

Alva talked to her about it, not showing how upset and worried she was. Her concern was for Renata and her inability to see how as a child she was an innocent in it all. The older women had used her for their own selfish ends. Yet at the same time she realized she must be careful about what she said about the girl's mother. If she condemned her it could alienate Renata further. It took all the diplomatic skills she had for her to soothe and comfort Renata and yet not condemn anyone in particular.

'I think we need to talk to your father,' Alva said. 'I know you think he won't understand but he will....'

'I know he'll understand but I don't want him to know what those women did ... don't you see how hurt he will be?'

'Renata, if your father had some idea about your mother he is not going to be hurt by learning even more about her, not now. That has all gone, it's in the long ago past. The thing that will really hurt him is if you keep this thing to yourself. He will want to help you, Renata, to show you how much he loves you.'

'Do you think so? He won't think I'm doing this to get back at you.'

'Of course not, Renata. Besides, that is not the reason, is it?'

Renata mulled over the question. 'I didn't want you back here, I told him that. I said if he got back with you he would lose me. . . .'

'Well he hasn't lost you, has he? You're here now and you are sharing your problems.'

'But he has enough to contend with . . . there's the threat to you. Isn't that enough for anyone?'

'We can handle both, Renata. The threat to me is a mystery that we might never solve, but we can solve your problem, that is what is important at this moment.'

'I can't tell him . . . but if you tell him—' She stopped. 'Then I won't be angry with you.'

Alva left them alone the next day. She asked Carlo to go with her to the mainland. It would have been good to have gone without him because she really needed the time alone, but that kind of foolishness, she knew, was forbidden to her for the moment.

She went to Primo, the small department store, and had coffee at the café. Afterwards she went around the store looking for gifts. Christmas was a week away and nothing had been organized. She could not remember a Christmas in Santa Caterina. Luca told her that during her last Christmas there she had been ill and in bed most of the time.

She thought of how he had taken her news about Renata. He had been so calm and accepting. She knew he had to be shocked and that he had to feel guilty too that he had not picked up on exactly how low his daughter's spirits had become. Yet he handled it perfectly. There was no anger – there was just acceptance and if he did not quite understand how his daughter had got to such a state, there was no condemnation or accusation.

Already wheels were put in motion and after the Christmas holiday, Renata had agreed to visit a psychiatrist with her father. At the moment she was adamant she could not return to university and so Luca had agreed to that as well.

Alva worried whether she could have helped Renata more when she had first been at the palazzo. Perhaps if she had not been so ill with the pregnancy then she would have worked harder at winning the girl around. Yet everything was strange to her at that time.

There were other things on her mind, too. As she looked at the cashmere sweater she thought would suit her stepdaughter, the momentous thing that had popped into her mind came to her again. Renata's unburdening herself, had, if not knocked it out of her mind, made it impossible to brood on it. It seemed so trivial in comparison to what the young girl had been through, yet it was not trivial. It answered a good few questions.

She had been with Luca a year. Their love affair, after an initial reluctance on her part, was known to everyone. At first she had not wanted people to know but Luca had persuaded her that they were both free of ties and they had nothing to be ashamed of.

She did not know whose fault it was – or maybe it was neither of their faults – it was just one of those things. She found herself pregnant. That was why he had married her.

Did Luca think she had tricked him into marriage? That she had used the age-old gamble – but it could have failed. He could have said he would accept the child but not matrimony. If only she could remember the whys and wherefores. Instead there was a void between knowing that he had had to marry her, and what he felt about it. She could not remember what was said, or even how he reacted. She just recalled that she was pregnant *before* the marriage.

Now with his attention being focused on his daughter she did not want to question him. It would come into her mind, it had to . . . these intervals now, when forgotten things came into her mind, were becoming more frequent. She had to be patient, but it was oh, so difficult, when she longed to know *everything*.

Arriving back at the palazzo she was met with silence. Nothing seemed to stir, there were not even any servants preparing dinner, or going about any tasks they had to do. Searching the downstairs she found each room empty. There was laughter from the kitchen so the staff had to be on afternoon break.

Going up the stairs she went first to Luca's bedroom. Opening the door she saw him, he had not heard her coming in. He was standing at the window looking out, a hand at the back of his neck as if he were suffering pain.

Murmuring his name she went to him. He turned and greeted her but there was a far-away look in his eyes – then, as she slid an arm on his shoulder, it was as if the gesture had chased it away and he smiled down at her.

'Did you have a nice day?'

'So, so, I was just buying some gifts. How are you, Luca, that is all that matters?'

'Oh,' he shrugged, 'you know. . . .'

'No, I don't, that's why I asked. Where's Renata?'

'Resting in her room. She's exhausted; all this self-flagellation has completely destroyed her. I knew she felt guilty about the crash – I thought it was because she had lived and Silvia had died. I had no idea she was blaming herself.'

'How could you know if she didn't tell you? But she

wanted to protect you, Luca.'

'Do you think I did not know? I wish I could have cared but Silvia and I were over, Alva, if we ever were something. I did not care what Silvia did, only that she was discreet. I had not realized what she was doing to Renata and that makes me feel miserable. That she was doing that to *her* daughter. . . .' Luca was angry for a moment, then, as if he realized that it was nothing to do with Alva, he shook the anger aside. 'I can help her now, and you were wonderful when she told you, Alva. You have not lost your gift for helping people out of tight spots . . . that is what Tony used to say. If you want out of a tight spot then Alva is the girl to see the way.'

'I don't know how,' she said. 'Luca. . . .'

'Yes?'

Yet how could she bring it up now when there were important things on his mind? The man was tormented about his daughter and yet she was going to go on about whether he felt forced to marry her or not. That was long ago and mattered only to herself.

'Nothing . . . I'm just pleased I could be there. But feeling about me as she did, I can't understand why Renata would have confided in me.'

'You were there when she needed someone. I think perhaps you two could have made a go of it were you given time and had things not been so . . . so miserable. . . .'

Ah, she thought, *miserable*. The key word, *miserable*. That was it, they were miserable in their marriage. That was why Renata had been unhappy; she had more than likely sensed that things were going badly between her father and his new wife. The young girl must have thought, here we go again . . . I am going to spiral down into hell once more!

Renata was quiet at dinner although Luca and Alva gave her all their attention. Now and again she came out of her monosyllabic answers to share something with them. Her liking for a movie or a book she had recently read. This little spurt of normality was a hopeful sign but they both knew it was too soon to settle back. Renata would need a lot of care and attention lavished on her if she were ever to feel worthy again.

'Renata, do you like to ride? Perhaps we could go riding tomorrow, would you like that?'

'Yes, perhaps,' the girl said, looking at her father, then back to Alva once more. 'But I do not ride as well as you, Alva.'

'I can't believe that.'

'No, it's true,' Luca said. 'You're a very skilled horsewoman, Alva. I remember you telling me that when you were at college and on break you used to take people on hacking holidays, as well as give riding lessons.'

'My, I hadn't realized I was that good.'

'Well, you are, and I will go with you, if it isn't raining. I don't like being out in the rain,' Renata said.

'I think I don't mind it,' Alva mulled it over in her mind. 'But being English I'm probably used to it.'

After Renata had gone to her room and Luca had announced he had some work to catch up on in the library, Alva decided to go up early and take a leisurely bath. She went past Renata's room and wondered whether to look in on her stepdaughter or if the girl was asleep. Putting her ear to the door she was surprised to hear the faint mumble of voices. It was not that Renata was on the phone because there were two voices although it was impossible to distinguish whose voices they were.

Curious and wanting to be certain that Renata was all right, Alva knocked on the door.

The girl called. 'Who is it?'

'It's Alva, Renata, are you all right.'

'I'm fine, Alva – *buona notte*.'

'*Buona notte*, Renata,' Alva answered. When she reached

her own room Alva had already made up her mind that Renata either was watching the television or had on the radio. Just because she did not have a television in her bedroom, it did not mean that Renata did not.

Renata came and found her the following morning to say she did not feel like riding but preferred to rest. Alva understood and after finding Carlo they went across to the stables and saddled their horses.

They took their usual ride down to the beach, racing the tide and enjoying the exhilaration. It was cold but fresh, with a sun that, although it was winter, had the hint of spring in it. 'I love the climate here,' she confessed to Carlo.

'I do also. It is better than in Firenze where it can be so cold in winter and so hot in summer.'

'You're from Firenze?' she asked.

'No, but I have worked there. Did you forget, Contessa, that I am from the north? I did tell you.'

'Of course you did. Sorry, I've had a lot on my mind. I just love Italy, I always have. I do remember I used to come here with my friend Chloe and her parents. They had a house in Chianti. . . .' She felt a warm rush. There a memory, something from her past had come naturally into her mind. 'Her father used to paint. He worked in advertising I think, yes I am sure, but in the summer at the house, he did what he dreamed of doing. Painting. We were so happy there, we had such freedom.'

'That is why you speak Italian so well, Contessa.'

'Well yes, I think so. They didn't offer Italian at the school I was at but I used to have private lessons with this wonderful old lady. Then the holidays with Chloe helped tremendously. I think I studied it at university too, but I can't remember exactly . . . it really is such a pain that I can't remember certain things and other things . . . I think it's the little things that I remember . . . the really important things. . . .' Her voice trailed away. However, it was not quite true for didn't she remember Luca, and he was important. Luca had been a momentous happening in her life. However, she said none of this to Carlo, realizing she had probably said too much anyway.

Arriving back at the stables she was surprised to see Renata coming from the pool house. She called her name but Renata either did not hear her or did not want to.

Leaving Carlo to help the stable boy unsaddle her horse she went to the pool house herself. Pushing open the door she looked inside. There was nothing of interest, just the huge empty swimming-room and pool furniture that was covered with a white cloth.

The dilapidated building next door looked as if someone had been and cleaned the windows, peering in she saw it had been tidied up since she had last been there.

Going to the door she pushed it open. It was completely empty and had indeed been swept clean. In various corners there was some blue chemical stuff; obviously it was to kill any rats. Thoughts of rats had her slamming the door and walking quickly across the courtyard.

In the hallway she all but bumped into Antonio. She rarely saw the man and was glad about that. Now, as she came on him again, she wondered how everyone had assumed that they were friends. Even now he was frigidly polite, merely inclining his head and murmuring her title. There was nothing there to hold on to, nothing about him awoke memories or that happy feeling when you met someone you really liked. Somehow she had given the wrong impression to someone about the man.

'Have you been to see the conte?' she asked.

'I delivered something for the conte,' the man said. 'I think the conte is visiting tenants.'

'Alone? He didn't take you with him?'

'Why should he do that, Contessa?'

'I don't know, I just thought he might have liked company.'

'He had Guido drive him today. Usually he goes alone; it is merely a social call to see if anyone has problems that they might like to share with him. He is very generous with his time.'

'Yes, I know that. Thank you.'

She turned and left him, swinging into the library. Sure enough, there was a parcel on the conte's desk. She went to examine it, not because she was curious but because she wanted to see what it was that Antonio had had to go and bring to her husband. However, the brown-paper-wrapped parcel gave no clues. Touching it, she discovered it was soft to the touch. Probably something that he had ordered from his tailor and Antonio had taken the launch to collect it from the mainland.

For a moment she looked around the library, seeing the shelves of books, some doubtless priceless. There were pictures on the opposite wall, even more of the severe-looking ancestors who graced the walls on the staircase. There was one she particularly liked; it was of a girl with long red hair, sitting on a balcony wearing some kind of medieval shift. Her luxurious hair was spread over her hand, her fingers splayed holding up a bunch of it, and obviously she was drying it in the sun. Alva knew of the tradition of Venetian ladies colouring their hair red and allowing it to dry this way, letting the sun naturally bleach their hair even lighter.

'It isn't an old painting.'

The voice caused her to leap up from the desk, but it was Renata.

'It is one of my mother's – see here is the signature – this "s", shaped like a snake. Appropriate don't you think?'

Alva ignored the statement. She felt as if somehow she was being set up to say something derogatory. It was an unsettling feeling but it lay heavily there in the centre of her stomach like an undigested piece of food. 'It's beautiful.'

'Yes, it is . . . hardly original – there are lots of paintings of this kind by old masters and their assistants. The bold ladies of Venice were a favourite subject.'

'I haven't seen a painting quite like that though.' Alva went closer to it. The oil painting was exquisite. What a clever and talented woman Luca's first wife must have been and yet he never spoke of her talent. He rarely spoke of Silvia, but that was hardly surprising given how she had been to him.

'My wife is dead,' he had told her when they had first gone out. But she had known that because she had checked with Tony whether he was married or not. 'She was killed in an automobile accident. . . .' Rarely after that had he spoken about Silvia.

Only as recently as yesterday had he hinted that the marriage was over and that he had not loved his first wife. A marriage for the family, he had said.

'She squandered her talent,' Renata went on. 'But it was her choice. You know what they did – what she did? Those paintings in the gallery, they are fakes you know. They sold the originals to a private buyer. Papa needed money so she copied them. Only an expert would tell the difference.'

'I thought they were genuine,' Alva said, showing her surprise. 'Your mother was a genius but I suppose it was her choice not to do anything about it.'

'She preferred to do what she did best,' Renata said, with a little laugh. 'And I guess you can guess what that was. Tell me, Alva don't you remember *anything* about when you were here before?'

The question was said so lightly that Alva felt she could have just shaken her head, but she had the feeling that more was implied. Again, it was that instinctive feeling that Renata was not saying exactly what she intended. That there was more behind everything she said just then. Something had happened to change her slightly. There was the faintest hint of that arrogance that the girl had had before her confession.

'No, I don't. I wish I did. . . .'

'You don't remember what happened when Alessandro died?'

Darts, straight for the heart. Little pinpricks that really hurt.

'No, Renata, I don't even remember Alessandro.'

'It's as well,' the girl said. 'You would suffer if you knew. You might even end up like me.'

Before she could say anything the girl ran from the room, swinging the door closed behind her, leaving Alva feeling weak and wounded and able only to sink into the chair.

End up like her? Renata was riddled with guilt, her opinion of herself torn to ribbons but Alva knew she would never be like that. Alva was certain, no matter what they all thought, that she had not deliberately thrown herself down the stairs. It was clear that Renata believed the story. It might even offer a slight balm to the girl's own guilt to know that her stepmother had done something wicked, too. Renata blamed herself for her mother's death; it would take wiser counselling than either she or Luca could offer to rid the girl of that feeling.

Feeling low, the exhilaration that her ride had brought about, fast ebbing, she ordered coffee and went to sit by the fire.

Claudia came at once, lightening Alva's mood slightly. Alva kept the woman chatting, for Claudia, if only she knew it, brought normality and light into Alva's life. The woman's warm and sunny personality did her more good than any pill would have done.

Before she finished her coffee Luca arrived. Immediately,

she ordered coffee for him and then went and lowered herself on to his knee, running a finger over the tiny lines that had formed across his brow. His worry lines she mentally called them.

'You shouldn't have to put up with all this, you have enough suffering of your own,' he said, meaning, of course, Renata.

'I'm glad to help – it helps take my problems from my mind and to tell the truth, my concern for Renata always chases away the terrible thing that happened to Rosa. Does that make me sound shallow, Luca?'

'You could never be shallow, Alva.'

She slid from his knee and waited until the coffee came, standing by the fireplace. Luca watched her, admiring the lean lines of her body in the riding breeches. The suede jerkin she wore left room for him to admire the rounded curve of her hips, clearly outlined in the tight-fitting clothes. He felt an overwhelming desire for her and recalled how that had always been there. Of course he had tried to drive it away, even at one time to pretend it never was, but his body and its reaction to the physical Alva, always betrayed him.

That was how it had been at first, purely physical and it was later that he realized how her personality soothed and pleased him too. Alva and he fitted together in every way which was why it had been so devastating when it had gone awry. She had done a wicked thing – but perhaps there was justification, everything then was unwinding between them. She had been making a nuisance of herself and he had tried to control her. Alva was not a woman who would accept control. Now, now things were different. They had a second chance. She had forgotten so much and was more . . . *malleable*.

Had he forgiven her? He was not sure that forgive was the right word but he had accepted that she could not help herself. That was a huge step for him to take mentally but he was making himself do that. One thing was for certain, when she had disappeared this time, when he knew she was in danger, it was as if his heart had been wrenched from inside him. He had never wanted *her* to be in danger.

'Luca,' she said, and her husky voice sounded troubled. She turned to look at him, pushing her hands into the pockets of her jerkin. 'Do you think it was because we had to get married that. . . .'

'*Cosa*?'

'With me being pregnant, we married and then. . . .'

He held up a hand. 'No, no, you are wrong, so wrong.'

'Luca? I had a dream; it came to me that we had to get married. I was pregnant and. . . .'

'No, *bella* . . . come here, sit beside me, you are confusing things.'

'I am?'

'Of course.'

She sat beside him, her mesmerizing green eyes looking deeply into his own. Her lashes were long and thick and far darker than her hair. He used to think that she dyed them only to find out that they were naturally dark, as were her well-shaped brows.

Nothing about her was artificial, that much he knew.

He smiled at her confusion. It was an easy thing for her to do with the muddled jumble that her mind was.

'No, it was not how you think. Let me explain to you. You thought you were pregnant at one time. I wanted us to marry right away but you wouldn't, you said it was all for the wrong reasons. You were so stubborn. Oh, my dear, you imagine that was Alessandro, that you were here such a short length of time?'

'Of course . . . but what happened? I know I'm confused but. . . .'

'Of course, you have partial recall of things, I think. The psychiatrist warned this might happen that things would not come back, if they ever did, all at once, but in fits and starts. Those were the words he used to me on the telephone, fits and starts – and I will tell you what happened:

'It was a mistake, you were not pregnant, it was just one of those things – you were late, and that was all. I told you there was no longer then any excuse for us *not* to marry. . . .'

She gazed up at him, trying to see beyond his words. He saw the light dawn; it came in her eyes, that warm glow.

'Yes, I wanted to marry you not for any reason of a child or because it was the thing to do. Oh, Alva, I wanted to be with you all the time. I wanted you to be my contessa and not my mistress.'

'Gosh,' she put a hand up to her forehead, pushing back the silvery fringe of hair. 'Then I was here longer than . . . than months.'

'Of course. You were here a little over two years.'

'I see.'

He drew her to him, resting her head against his chest. Her hair smelt of meadow sweet, it always had and against his lips, felt like spun silk.

'You must really think me stupid.'

'Alva, of course I don't. You can't help your memory loss. But if things come back to you I want you to promise to come to me right away, find me, call me, it is important that you don't go down the wrong path.'

'I promise and today something else came to me. . . .'

She told him what she had remembered of summer holidays in Chianti with Chloe's parents. How they had always had the most perfect time. She even remembered the name of the lady who had first taught her Italian. Maria Granelli. 'I remember how her name sounded like music. . . .'

'There, little bits come and stay and more will come, I am

sure of it. . . .' He bent his head and captured her ear, kissing it gently. She whispered a sigh of pleasure. Lifting her head, she slid fully on to his knee, wrapping herself around him, seeking out his mouth.

He thought of the day ahead, of the appointments he had. The people he had to see, the problems that needed sorting out. He said to her. 'To the devil with the day. . . .'

CHAPTER NINE

CHRISTMAS came and went quietly. Alva had ordered a tree and dressed it. She made arrangements for the Christmas lunch and bought gifts for the servants and for Renata.

Renata moved like a girl in a trance through most of it, saying little and spending a lot of time alone but she was never unpleasant any more. Her quietness was worrying; it was as if she was now nursing all her problems to herself. She refused resolutely to be coaxed into sharing her thoughts. She had had two sessions with a psychiatrist and had more booked. She admitted that it helped but said nothing else. However, she ate, although sparingly, so she obviously was not starving herself.

Trusting Claudia, Alva had instructed only her to clean Renata's room. She would report anything that looked bloodied to her. Alva knew that once trusted, Claudia would not betray that trust by telling the other servants about Renata's cutting herself.

Claudia had reported that everything was quite normal and she did, when certain that the girl was away from her room, give it a thorough search.

Alva explained. Claudia assured her that she understood only too well.

New Year swept in quietly. No guests came to stay but

Renata joined them for dinner on New Year's Eve and even went to Midnight Mass in the village. It was a crisp, star-filled evening and they stood in the square listening to the bells sing in the New Year. Alva hoped they were chiming in better things.

When Luca said he had to go away for more than a couple of days Alva felt miserable. He did not ask her to accompany him and she thought she knew why. He wanted her to keep an eye on Renata. It was Alva and Carlo who went with the girl to the psychiatrist and brought her back. Renata had regained enough spirit to declare she would not go and be an in-patient anywhere and would not listen to reason on the matter. It had been a surprise to learn that the request for Alva to go with her had come from Renata. For some reason she did not want her father involved with her treatment and refused even to talk to him about it.

'I think she might be a little ashamed, as if she should be!' Luca said. 'I wish she would realize that I blame her for nothing.'

'She's a little unstable at the moment, Luca, you can't expect rational behaviour, but I admit it seems odd that she wants me of all people to accompany her.'

He looked at her for a long moment, as if pondering whether to say anything or not. Instead of persuading him to speak, Alva went and sat in the armchair, looping her fingers together nervously, feeling inside her a terrible tension and not knowing the reason why.

'She sees you as someone who has been there, Alva.'

'But I never—' She stopped and recognized the reason she felt tense. Of course, her *supposed* suicide attempt. That would continue to raise its ugly little head until she remembered the truth of what happened. However, the momentary anger evaporated. How could she blame Luca for believing that when he had *so-called* evidence of what she had done? She had no memory so how could she explain it away. Besides, if it meant that Renata thought she had an ally so much the better. At least Alva felt she could be useful on some level.

Yet when Luca left she brooded through the long night, barely sleeping, tormented by the fact that he still, after their coming together so blissfully, believed that she would be so wicked as to try to take her own, as well as their baby's life. All the excuses in the world did not take the bitter taste from her.

She felt weary the next day, yet when Renata came to breakfast her stepdaughter was oddly bouncy. Was it her? Was the lassitude she felt making her see things about Renata that had not been apparent to her before? Perhaps she was just run down and by comparison Renata seemed to be lively.

Later in the day she knew that was not the case. Renata was showing all the signs of being on a mental high. Talking and moving about restlessly, making plans, only to discard them within half an hour. She would go back to university – she would not. She would stay here and help her father manage things. She had a talent for managing. Perhaps she would take a business course – but that would be boring, wouldn't it?

Tired as she was, Alva watched her stepdaughter carefully. Renata said she would take the launch to the mainland to do some shopping and that Alva, who looked really ill, need not bother to come with her. Antonio would take her in the boat and bring her back. Antonio was good company – surely Alva remembered that! Alva could not remember anything about Antonio in the past but what she did know was that he had lied about her, that he was not good company and that she did not like him one little bit. However, she said none of these things to Renata, if Renata was feeling cheerful enough to go shopping then Alva was happy for her.

Yet the feeling persisted after the girl had gone that Renata was a little too cheerful. It was way out of character. Going to the computer she checked up on the symptoms of the medication she knew Alva to be on. There was nothing about the chemicals giving the user a high. In fact they were a very mild anti-depressant.

Worried and uncertain, Alva put in a call to Renata's psychiatrist. He was friendly and humorous. He had a good rapport with Alva but whether he would talk about Renata she was unsure. He came on the line and was as cheerful and charming as ever. His first question, although she was not strictly his patient, was how was she doing and had she remembered anything? She told him, as she liked him, about her confused dream. Her really believing that they had had to get married because she was pregnant, when that was not the case. 'Well, it was nearly right, Alva. Your case fascinates me, you know, I wonder if you would like to try hypnosis sometime.'

'Tried it, it didn't work.'

'Well, maybe now when there are openings in your mind. Anyway, think about it and let me know. Now I imagine you want to talk about Renata?'

'I feel mean doing this, Dottore, but Renata seems suddenly so cheerful. Almost as if she is going through a little high, you know what I mean?'

What a stupid question, she thought, if anyone knew about highs and lows it had to be a psychiatrist.

'Do you think she has nothing to be happy about? Or that perhaps she is getting better?'

'It's come all at once. Yesterday she hardly spoke to anyone, today she is going to change the world – slight exaggeration but you know what I mean.'

'Sounds a little strange. I tell you what, Alva, tell her I called to change her appointment. Can you bring her in tomorrow?'

'She might hit the roof, but I'll try. Thank you, Dottore.'

When Renata arrived home she was carrying four bags of shopping and Antonio was following her with some more bags. Alva came across them in the hall and they were laughing conspiratorially, so much so that Alva suspected that Renata was slightly drunk.

'Renata, you look as though you've had a good time.' Alva kept her voice level, managing a smile and a brisk manner.

'We had a fantastic time!'

'*We*? Did you meet some friends?'

'Er . . . of course, what else?' Renata dropped her bags in the hall and told Antonio to do the same. 'The servants will bring them to my room later.'

Then she turned and skipped off into the drawing-room. Alva looked across at Antonio. He was putting the bags neatly together at the side of the hall, anticipating that someone could fall over them if they were left where Renata dropped them.

'And the *signorina* met friends where?' she asked him.

He shrugged with that faint arrogance he had. 'No idea,' he murmured. Then inclining his head and muttering, 'Contessa,' he turned to go away.

'Where did she go, where did you leave her?'

'At the port, Contessa, and really if you want to know I would suggest you ask Renata,' he said smoothly.

'Signorina Mazareeze, I think you mean.'

The man whispered something under his breath. Alva knew that if he were English it would have been 'whatever' – it had that touch of insolence about it.

'That will be all, Antonio,' she said coldly, answering his stare with one of her own. She waited in the hall until he had turned and gone out through the front door. Pouring invectives on his head in her mind, she went in search of someone to see to Renata's bags before seeking out the girl herself.

*

'What did you buy?' Alva asked pleasantly.

'Clothes – lingerie, girl's stuff – why, you want to look in my bags?' Renata was back to her impudent self. It was in the way she stood, the arrogant way she tossed her dark hair.

'Of course not, I just wondered. Who did you meet?'

'It's none of your business who I go to meet, Alva. Please don't overstep the mark. I'm almost nineteen not twelve!'

'I was just curious, Renata. Have your little secrets if you want. The main thing is that you had a good time.'

Renata pulled a face rudely, and then, thinking better of it, said. 'I did enjoy myself, it was great.'

Alva thought it was probably not the right time to tell her about the psychiatrist but she went ahead anyway. Surprisingly, Renata accepted that the dottore had changed his appointment and did not even question it.

'It's OK, we can do that. I think I might wear one of my new outfits. Red – scarlet – trousers and top.'

'That sounds nice and cheerful. I love red for winter.'

'Yes – perhaps I'll wear a white scarf and then I will look like a leftover from Christmas.'

'I think you'll look fine. Did you eat?'

'Yes, I won't want dinner. I think I'll go to my room. Have one of the servants bring up my stuff and have someone call me in the morning. *Ciao*, Alva.'

Alva hesitated, debating whether she should try to persuade Renata to stay with her a little while. Thinking it would be kinder to try to talk to her she suggested it, but Renata shook her head.

'No, really, I have things I want to do. My clothes, I want to try them on and put them away. Besides, there's an interesting programme on the television I want to watch.'

'OK, if you're sure. Would you like me to send up a tray – tea perhaps. . . .'

'Alva, do stop fussing. I'm not a child, if I want anything I can ring down for it.'

'Of course you can, I just thought—'

'What did you think, Alva, that you would *mother* me? Heaven forbid I'd have you for a mother!'

'Well, thank you for that, Renata. I wasn't actually seeing myself as your mother. I was seeing myself as a friend.'

Alva hurt inside. The little arrows that Renata managed to fire in her direction always managed to penetrate the veneer she put up. It was as if the girl knew that underneath her outward appearance, Alva was vulnerable and still raw from her recent experiences.

'Hah,' Renata said, dismissing Alva with a wave of her hand. 'Don't be that either. It is enough that you are my father's wife. We don't have to be friends.'

So, not even when I was the one you came to with your problems. That faced your father for you. Things had not changed; Renata would never like her – or was that strictly true? Were these mood fluctuations that Renata so clearly displayed the effects of her own trauma?

'All right, Renata, have a nice night.'

Alva turned away. She went towards the French doors – a walk in the cool air would do her good.

'I don't mean it,' Renata said. 'I just can't stop it.'

Alva turned to look at Renata; the girl's face was full of confusion. 'Are you all right?'

Now she looked angry, as if the words had slipped out and she wanted to recall them.

'Yes, take no notice of me.' Renata swung herself around, almost staggering out of the room. She slammed the door behind her, and the echo of it reverberated all around the house.

It is her psychological state, Alva thought, although not certain she should be relieved. She vowed to have a word with the psychiatrist on that too. These mood swings were getting out of hand.

Later going to her own room to bathe before dinner, the sound of loud music drifted along the passage from Renata's room. The thud of the base thrust out through the door at full volume. Hesitating for a second, Alva decided not to go and ask her to turn it down. Once in her own room she knew she would barely hear it, yet it seemed worrisome that Renata needed the music so loud, it had to be bad for her hearing. *I am getting to be an old fuddy-duddy,* Alva thought, climbing into her bathtub, *to worry about things like that. It's what youngsters do and I was probably just as bad . . . if I could remember I would know it.*

Claudia said, 'The *signorina* is not in her room, Contessa. Her bed is unmade, of course, and her bathroom has been used, but she is not there. I cannot think where she is.'

Alva checked her watch. It was ten-thirty and she had told Renata that they would leave at eleven. 'She must have gone for a walk, Claudia; I'll go to see if I can find her.'

Outside it was a bright sunny day. There was a sliver of warmth in the sun too and it made Alva hesitate. She paused to raise her face to the sun's rays and thought of what was before them. Warm, gentle spring days. She loved the spring in Italy, the flowers, the birds, the scent of jasmine carried on mild, soft winds. Glorious. Yes, she did remember those days and the memory filled her with pleasure.

She set off briskly. First she went to the stables; the boys were working but they had not seen the *signorina*. She walked around the pool, looking for signs of someone having used the pool, although it was highly unlikely that Renata would have used it. Her stepdaughter had told Alva that she thought she was mad for swimming out of doors in winter, even if the pool was heated.

Crossing the yard, she hesitated a moment before opening the doors to the storage rooms adjacent to the indoor pool. There was some stuff in there that had not been there before. Black bin bags neatly folded. Assuming it was garden waste, she closed the door, going to the old pool house. That was empty. She called, knowing it was fruitless. There was no reason for Renata to be in there.

Wandering through the gardens, she passed the two gardeners clearing away some pruned roses and shrubs. To her question, they too said they had not seen the *signorina*.

The one place she had not been to was the summerhouse. It was the place Alva often went to, not to go into the summerhouse but to put flowers on the grave of Alessandro, or sometimes just to sit and wonder what had happened that had robbed him of his life, before it had had a chance to begin.

Although Renata never spoke of Alessandro, she had thrown out dark hints about what Alva had done, but that was not to say she would not visit the little grave. Alessandro was after all, her half-brother and the girl, troubled as she was, might have deeper feelings than she imagined.

The doors to the summerhouse were closed. Renata was not sitting on the little wrought iron seat where Alva often sat. Curiously, the shutters at the windows of the summerhouse were drawn. Odd that they would be, Alva thought, for they were always thrown back so that the interior of the little house could gain benefit from sunlight to keep it well aired.

The handle on the door turned easily and silently, before she pushed open the door she stepped back. She heard a faint deep moaning. Renata, hiding in misery . . . but it was not a girl's voice. Renata had a fairly high-pitched tone.

Thoughts tumbled into her mind, it could be a trick . . . a trick against her. She needed Carlo with her, she should not

. . . slowly she partly pushed open the door, peering into the opening.

She felt sickened. As quietly as she opened it she closed the door, turned around and sped into the house. Going directly into the library she slammed the French doors closed, leaning back against them. Her whole body was trembling with disgust and rage and an inexplicable desire to do someone harm. The image came into her mind again, hard and cruel and stirring up the rage until she felt herself slipping out of control. Renata and *him* . . . Renata on her knees. . . .

'I can't deal with this,' she murmured to herself. The girl was nineteen but she was so mixed up . . . the man had to have some control over her. It was not love; he was using her, that sad and vulnerable young girl.

Regaining control of herself, she stood, her hand still shaking, even as she picked up the telephone. She would sack him, order him from the property. Yet had she the right to do that? Would she be believed anyway, would it be a case of a trusted employee's word over hers, collaborated doubtless by Renata?

The telephone seemed to screech out to her, its bell thundering in her mind. She picked it up. '*Pronto.*'

'*Ciao, cara,* how are you?'

Luca!

'Are you all right? Are you not speaking to me?'

The words would barely come out, she felt herself choking. 'Luca, I need you to come home.'

'Well, that is why I am calling. I shall be home tonight. What is it?' Suddenly his tone changed, becoming urgent.

'I'm all right but I need you. I really need you, Luca.'

'Something is wrong. I'm on my way, I should be there. . . .' There was a moment's silence as he checked his watch. 'In about two hours, I can take a private jet.'

'Please do that, Luca, *please*!'

All thoughts of going to the psychiatrist had gone from her mind by the time Renata bounced into the room. Her eyes were wide and sparkling, she had that giddiness that Alva had recognized yesterday.

'He called, he has had to cancel,' Alva lied.

'Damn him. The stupid man, he has made a mess of my day.'

'I can't see how that can be, Renata, I think you can find lots to do.'

'You think? I'll go to find Antonio; he can take me to the mainland.'

'I wouldn't do that if I were you.'

'Why not?'

'Because your father is coming home, in fact he'll be here in two hours.'

'So? Why should I care, he only wants to be with you.'

'That's not true, Renata.'

'Isn't it? Well I'm still going to the mainland.'

'You can go but you will have to ask Carlo to take you. Your father has something for Antonio to do, Renata. He especially asked me to make sure he was here.'

'Oh, well, he'll have to be here then, won't he.'

Renata turned and bounced out of the room, following her, Alva was relieved to see the girl running up the stairs. She waited at the bottom until she heard the bedroom door slam.

CHAPTER TEN

LUCA was staring at her. Her insides shrivelled, it was as if someone was pouring icy water down her spine. She knew that in a moment she would crumble and start to tremble. She knew that look, remembered it from another time – but why he had looked at her like that she could not remember? He was at once the Conte Luca San Giovanni Mazareeze. He was not her husband, or the man she loved. He was someone she did not know and – more important – did not want to.

But she was wrong, the hard stare was looking through her; she saw her mistake immediately because he came to her and pulled her tenderly into his arms, holding her to him.

'You looked so pale, I thought you were going to faint,' he murmured.

'No, I'm fine, I just find it. . . .'

'I know,' he murmured. 'Thank you,' he added. 'Sit down. . . .' He led her to the sofa and gently made her sit, then he crossed to his desk and lifted up the telephone. It rang out a long time and then must have gone to voicemail for he said, in a voice so level and smooth. 'I need to see you right way.' Then put down the phone.

'He has his mobile switched off. I wonder what he is up to,' Luca's eyes narrowed.

He was holding himself in check; she could sense that and even see it in the stiff way he held himself.

'What are you doing to do?'

'I think I am going to kill him.'

'Luca?' Fearfully she looked at him, was half out of her seat when his shaking of his head made her sit back down.

'Not literally, although my ancestors would have cut his throat without a second's thought.'

'And Renata?'

He ran a hand through his hair. 'I am going to try to persuade her to go into the clinic. She desperately needs help, if these mood swings are as you say. . . .'

'They are just a little more than the usual girl thing.'

'She should be past the girl thing, as you call it, she is almost twenty. When I think of how vulnerable she is . . . *per Dio*, Alva, I cannot wait here; I must find that *pezzo di merda*.'

'I'm coming with you; don't say no, I need to be with you, Luca.'

'You want to prevent me doing something bad to him. *Cara*, you could not stop me even if you tried, but come then . . . if you will feel better. . . .'

The last place they went was the storage room. No one had seen Antonio – Luca even sent Guido to look for the man in the village. Inside the storage room they saw that the door to the steps that led to the cellar was open. Luca crossed to it, staring down.

Glancing around the area nervously, Alva saw that the black plastic bin bags had gone. Luca pulled on the switch and the stairs were illuminated.

He called down. 'Antonio . . . Antonio. . . .' His voice bounced back to him. Standing close to him Alva could smell a damp mustiness wafting up the stairs. Luca started to descend.

'Stay here,' he commanded to Alva, 'these steps are dangerous and you could easily fall. . . .'

Nervously, Alva stood on the top step, watching as Luca descended carefully. There was no handrail and the stairs were steep and spiraled down, rather than went straight.

She could hear his footsteps striking each stone step. Then the darkness was illuminated some more so she guessed he had reached the cellars and the passageway that Claudia had told her about, and put on a light.

'Luca, you aren't going to the shore, are you . . . Luca?'

'Of course not, why would I do that? There is nothing there but a grim passage to the fort, no one would be there. There is no one here. Besides as I told you it is dangerous, it could collapse at any moment.'

She heard him coming back up. She stepped back, nervously glancing around the empty space. This place gave her the creeps. It was not just her fear of rats. She knew the creatures had to be there as there was poison in every corner, but it was something more. It was an irrational fear but a fear nevertheless.

'Let's get out of here,' she said, when he came back. Taking up his hand she urged him across towards the door.

'There's nothing to be frightened of,' Luca said reassuring her.

'I'm scared of rats.'

'There are no rats here, why would they be here. There is nothing to eat.'

'But there's rat poison, there in the corners. . . .'

'I don't know why that would be,' Luca said. 'Come, I know how you feel about such things.' He put an arm around her, going at her pace to leave the room. They emerged in the weak sunlight to see Guido coming back in the Fiat. 'He is not in town, Conte. No one has seen Antonio.'

Just then, Luca's mobile phone rang out. He put it to his ear saying. '*Pronto*?' He nodded at Guido and then said into the phone. 'I need to see you right away, Antonio, come to the house . . . no, wait a minute, can you come to the storeroom by the old pool house?'

After instructing Guido to go back to whatever he was doing, he slipped the mobile into the pocket of his jacket. 'He is coming; he says he was down at the boat, that he had his phone off by accident. As if I would believe that.'

'We looked at the boat,' Alva murmured.

'Yes. Perhaps he was with Renata.'

'In the house? But he could not have been in the house. Renata would have told him you were coming back and surely he would not risk being caught?'

'He need not have been caught,' Luca said. 'My daughter's room has a passage. It runs between one of the guest bedrooms and her room.'

'My God! I heard voices one night, I thought it was the television. I've been so stupid.'

'No, *cara*, I am the stupid one.'

Renata was hysterical, shouting and screaming. Had her father not held her wrists Alva knew she would have struck him. Words spewed out of her mouth that made Alva's blood run cold. Her stepdaughter was out of control.

'I love him, I love him!' she cried. 'You bastard, doing that to me, taking him from me.'

'He doesn't love you, Renata. He was using you.'

'He wasn't, you have no right, I'm not a child!'

'Then stop behaving like one. Where is your self-respect?'

Wrong thing to say, Alva thought, she doesn't know what that is just now. Her opinion of herself is so low she would not care even if she understood. Yet she could not bring herself to condemn him. Luca had to be in shock and feeling shameful, too. This was his daughter and he had not known what was going on. Yet how could he have known anything? Obviously Renata was adept at deceit, and her lover was a past master at it as well.

'Now listen to me!' Luca urged. But she screamed over his calm words, blaming everyone but Antonio himself.

Her angry words rang down Alva's ears, she put up her hands to stop them – her head was starting to spin, it was as if her brain was an out of control traffic light – she actually saw lights before her eyes, flash, flash, jumbled memories colliding inside her head.

She cried out, above their din. 'Stop it, please, both of you I. . . .'

She was lying on the bed; the room was semi-dark and there were murmured concerned voices. She opened her eyes, aware of the pain throbbing away at her head.

There was Luca, whispering with a man. Squeezing her eyes, she saw through the dimness that it was Alfredo Martino, the kindly doctor. Luca must have brought him from the mainland.

As she struggled to sit up she made a rustling sound, and both men turned and hurried to her side.

'Alva?' Doctor Martino smiled at her, taking her wrist in his hand, feeling for her pulse. 'How are you now?'

'I'm all right, what happened?' she a ran a hand through her tousled hair. 'I was downstairs and then. . . .'

'You fainted, more than that, you passed out. *Cara*, I've been so worried about you.'

Luca sat on the bed.

'It was the noise . . . Renata yelling, you shouting – it was like an explosion in my head.'

'I'm sorry, I am so sorry, *cara*.'

'No, not just you, not just you and Renata, there was a noise in my head, voices, rushing sounds, pictures . . . as if I was going insane.' Eagerly she looked at Alfredo, wanting a medical answer.

'You are the sanest person I know, Alva,' he murmured quietly. 'Tell me, what do you know, Alva, what have you seen?'

She bit her lip, breathing deeply. 'I'm not sure if I'm dreaming, I don't know what's real or not . . . I think it's real,' she looked at Luca. 'San Remo,' she said. 'The bougainvillea was out, purple and scarlet; it hung down the walls, close to our little balcony. We drank champagne, just the two of us . . . it was our honeymoon. I was a spring bride.'

'*Cara, cara. . . .*'

'I will wait outside; I think you have things to share.'

'Go and have a drink, anything you want Alfredo . . . I will send Guido to you. . . .'

'Don't worry, Conte, I know where you keep the best Scotch.'

Alva moved her legs restlessly against the silk sheet, unsure of feelings and thoughts and long buried memories. It was all there but jumbled somehow. She remembered the past but it was out of order. Inside her head was like a damaged DVD that played well and then jumped and you missed a whole section. She said as much to Luca. He said nothing, just watched her carefully as if unsure what she would say or do. Hardly surprising because she did not know that either.

'Where is Renata?'

'In her room, don't worry. Alfredo gave her a calming draft. She isn't sleeping but resting, she's very quiet but she's all right. One of the maids is sitting with her. I also locked the passageway from the other side. Just in case she decides to run away.'

'This has been a terrible day,' Alva muttered, realizing that it was an understatement.

She didn't want to think about the scene between Renata

and her father. It was too painful. Her mind slipped back to Antonio, she could see his smirking face. His arrogance, out in the open now and not hidden. He blamed Renata, said the girl had come on to him. Renata, having so little self-confidence, Alva thought, was hardly likely to come on to anyone! Believing herself worthless, the girl would not have thought anyone would love or like her. Of course now Alva knew even more than that initial thought. Things had come storming back to her.

It was not a recent thing, this *affair* with Antonio; it had not started when Renata had come back so damaged from university. She had seen them before; years ago . . . her eyes filled with tears. *Alessandro, I should have taken more care of you, little one, there in my tummy, feeling you were safe.*

'*Cara*, what is it?'

'It was my fault, the stairs . . . everything!' A huge sob choked its way out of her. Luca was there, holding her soothing her. It was all in the past, he said, and it was gone now.

'But it will never be gone, Luca. It was my fault but not the way you think. . . .'

'What do you mean?'

'Oh, Luca.' Letting the tears fall was a relief of sorts. Had she cried for Alessandro when she discovered what had happened? But no, Luca and what he believed had driven all that out of her. Inside she had felt cold and bitter and wanted only to put as much distance between them as she could. She had thought, at that moment, all those years ago, that she hated him, truly hated him. She loathed Renata and as for Antonio, she had no words. How could his daughter not have told Luca? She had to have known what had happened.

Antonio, so cocky then in the past, just as he had been only that very afternoon. There he was, coming out of Renata's room, boldly swaggering in front of her and knowing that she had seen where he had come from. Maybe he even knew what she had seen, in the summerhouse – the summerhouse that place again that held so many dark, bitter secrets.

'How dare you!' That is what she had said, challenging him instead of letting him go, not even thinking of finding Luca. Why not? The answer was simple and at the same time pitiful: she had not wanted to alienate Renata even more and yet what a wrong decision that had turned out to be.

She had been standing just at the top of the stairs. 'Get out of my way, bitch,' he had dared to say, in fractured English. 'You won't tell him . . . or else.'

'You think not? You're very mistaken. . . .'

And then he had raised his hand, she had watched it, almost hypnotized by the slowness of the movement and then it hit her chest, only lightly but she went down, down and down her head striking the cool marble, knocking her unconscious, not even able to try to stop herself, having no ability to grab the banister . . . down, down, down. . . .

'What is it?'

'You won't believe me,' she said, and felt the tears start to tremble against her lashes.

'I will, I swear.'

She shook her head. 'You believed Antonio before; you took his word against mine.'

'*Cara*, you told me nothing. You would not talk about what happened. There was no option but to believe Antonio and—' He hesitated, a hand went out and gently brushed back her fringe of hair, his fingers cool against her overheated forehead.

'You see, I did not want to cause trouble when you came back but, forgive me, you see Renata also confirmed his story.'

'Renata! But Renata was not there, she was in her room, she did not *see* anything.'

'You believe she lied for Antonio, but why would he say

such a thing? You can see how difficult it was for me.'

'Yes and no. I don't remember not telling you what happened, maybe I did not remember . . . was that the start of my memory going, that push down the stairs? Had I already started to forget things then?'

'What push down the stairs? *Cara*, you must tell me what you mean! What is it you have remembered?'

'Oh, Luca . . . Renata and Antonio, it was not a new thing, it was going on when I was here first. I caught him coming out of her room. I . . . I had seen them in the summerhouse, making. . . .' Making love? No, she could not describe it like that, more like having sex, she thought, but she added the softer version for his benefit. 'He pushed me down the stairs because I said I would tell you. It is as simple as that. Antonio killed our baby.'

She recognized all the words he used, and turned her head away from the violence that spilled out of him, flinching from the anger, afraid as he paced the room.

'It's all come at the wrong time,' she said, trying to soothe him. 'So many things happening all at once, I'm sorry Luca.'

'You have nothing to be sorry for. But one consolation, please . . . Renata was not part of the pushing; you swear she was not there?'

'No, it was just him and me. I swear it. Maybe he told her I threw myself down the stairs, asked her to collaborate his story. She was a young girl, who imagined herself in love, whatever he told her she would believe. And it was easy to believe wasn't it? I was so miserable; I was out of control myself.'

'And that is something else. Maybe you were feeling so ill through no fault of your own, have you thought of that?'

'You mean Antonio put something in my food to make me so ill? Why would he do that?'

'I don't know, to keep you tied to the house. Afraid that you would find out about him and Renata. If you remember, I was away a lot. I had a problem with some properties on the mainland.'

'I don't remember that ... but I will ... now that my memory is opening up, one day it will settle down and I will remember everything. . . .'

The palazzo became very quiet. Renata haunted her bedroom and seldom came out. Her psychiatrist came to see her and he stayed two nights, spending most of his days with Renata, and then went into the library to talk to Luca.

Renata was in unforgiving mood; her life was in ruins, she told the psychiatrist, and she would never get over what had happened to her.

Luca would not bend and Alva admired him for it. There was nothing more difficult than tough love but he believed that was the only way to get her out of her present mood.

It was only a mild surprise when the psychiatrist reported that she had been taking cocaine. No need to ask who had given it to her. She was not totally addicted, he said, because she had not been on it that long, only since she had been home. The highs and lows made sense to Alva.

'I should have recognized it,' she told Luca, 'because I've seen it before.'

'Of course, Tony liked to do drugs,' Luca said.

'Yes, he did, Tony would try anything. Did I tell you that? I seem to think I did.'

'Of course but I knew anyway because he asked me if I wanted some charley. I didn't even know what he meant!'

'You wouldn't. Oh, Luca why have you had all this visited on you? You don't deserve it.'

'Not me, *cara*, you. Why have you had all this visited on *you*? All these things that have been happening have not been because that *coglione* seduced my daughter. There has to be more to it than that, you are sure you don't remember anything else?'

'No . . . nothing . . . there are gaps, so perhaps there is something else. I don't think Antonio was trying to have me killed. Do you? I mean . . . because of what he was doing to Renata? Hardly likely, and he went easily enough. And what was it that Rosa wanted? Why was she killed? There is a lot we don't know and I have a horrid feeling it is in here' – she tapped her forehead – 'somewhere.'

'Or someone thinks you know something that you don't. Oh, *cara* . . . I'm so sorry.'

'It's not your fault Luca. And I'm not sorry to be here, with you. . . .'

'We will succeed, won't we?'

'How do you mean?'

'You and I?'

'If you want us to succeed then we will, Luca.' She looked at him, he looked worried and she knew he was tortured by what had happened to Renata, as if he blamed himself, when there was nothing he could have done. Renata had not told him of her own troubles but sank into a terrible despair on her own. It had been Antonio who had taken advantage of her vulnerability.

Her heart opened up – it was all right when things were normal pretending that she was not in love with Luca, tucking her real feelings away, waiting for him to say something but now . . . now she understood why he would not say how he really felt. He was afraid of making her feel that he was tying her down. The bird had flown and might want to fly again. . . .

'Luca,' she took up his hand. 'Luca, I love you so much.'

The 'oh,' was dragged up from the very pit of him. She had never heard such a savage cry of agony. 'I don't deserve it,' he muttered, holding her to him and then she knew, realized in that holding just how precious she was to him.

'I never stopped loving you, Alva. I tried to chase it away with words of hate and I never completely succeeded. *Cara, sel il mio piu' grande amore. . . .'*

It was very dark in the room. Alva awoke suddenly because something disturbed her sleep. Luca was working downstairs; she had left him there as she had felt exhausted. Everything that had happened had seemed to drain the life from her. Renata – Antonio – most of all, the memories that tripped like a fast-running, flickering film into her mind, overwhelming her.

All the questioning she had to do of herself, was that real, a genuine memory, or an imaginary incident? Most of the time Luca could supply the answers but there were some things in her past that even he did not know about.

'Luca?' Something had definitely woken her, a soft footfall, a creak; stretching out a hand she reached for the lamp. 'Luca?' she called out again, her finger found the switch, clicked it on and the bedroom's blackness was pierced by soft pink light and then . . . blackness. Something over her head blocking out the warm glow of light. It was a rough kind of sacking bag, the smell of it musty and dank. It felt cold against her face and coated in slimy damp mould. The sack covered her from head to below her shoulders, a strap of sorts holding it in place at her throat. She struggled and tried to scream but hands grabbed her arms, tying them behind her, she was being dragged from the bed, her feet landed on the floor . . . she wriggled, terrified in the black nightmare . . . wondering if it was a nightmare, just for a moment, until a sharp little pain proved the reality, a needle, softly sliding into the flesh of her arm.

Bile rose up in her throat, she would choke . . . waves of heat broke out over her body, the thin shift of silk clinging to her. Her feet left the floor, her body was being thrown … down … down stairs … but no, just as the terror started to mount she slipped away into nothingness. …

She came to slowly. It was very cold. She moved her foot, her ankles were bound now, but her toes were touching something soft and damp. There was a sound, a rushing, folding sound … she listened … it was almost drowned out by the fearful clamouring of her heart. God! It was the sea. She was trussed like a dozen unwanted puppies, in a sack, ready to be thrown in the water. The sea … the element she loved … yet where she had almost died before. 'I don't want to die like this,' she thought hysterically, trying to move – but no, she was too well trussed even to wriggle, just able to move her toes against the sand.

A voice then. There was something familiar about it, but not in its tone. 'What are you doing, you *testa di cazzo*?'

'I'm getting rid of her.' That was Antonio; she knew his voice, that high-pitched slightly effeminate tone. But who was the other? Where had she heard *that* voice before?

'I told you to leave it.'

'So, who are you telling me what to do? I want her out of the way.'

'You know what, you're trouble, and you're too emotional.'

'What's that supposed to mean?'

'You think too much about what happens to *you* and not what happens to the job. So she upset you, so what? She knows nothing … she can't even remember her name properly. She gets confused all the time.'

'You think so?'

'I know so. And what can she tell *him* anyway that he isn't aware of. I told you when you tried to get rid of her before, leave her be, she's nothing and the conte will never forgive you if you hurt her. He will hunt you down like the *coglione* you are. We stick to business, that's the arrangement, nothing else. And why were you carrying on with the kid again? I told you to leave her too! You can only push him so far and then. . . .'

The voice, sounding commanding now, someone she knew . . . Italian . . . but with a slight accent, the man on the boat . . . but no, not him, only the accent a little like his. She lay still, she could hear her heart clanging away, and feared they would hear it too.

'Who do you think you are, who put you in charge all of a sudden? You can't order me what to do. I can please myself.'

The man ignored that, he went on saying. 'It was the same with Rosa. *Sei pazzo*! No need to kill her!'

'Oh yeah, well Rosa was going to tell *her* everything.' Antonio kicked her, she knew it was him, his voice was the nearest, it took every ounce of courage not to cry out; it was not a gentle kick. But if they discovered she had come round it might make it worse.

'Like what everything? You idiot, Rosa would not have told her anything – it was just business between two stupid bitches.'

'She was going to tell her whose kid Renata was and other stuff. . . .'

'*E allora*? Who cares whose kid Renata is?'

'I care. I don't want to marry a penniless bitch.'

'Emotional, like I said. You think you're going to marry Renata, *never* . . . you're a liability, Antonio, always have been, always will be. *Ciao, baby*!'

Against the gentle swish of the sea in the darkness of night the gun sounded so loud. Not a crack but a thunderous noise that echoed around the bay. She was so close to it it hurt her ears.

'Oh my God,' she thought, 'Luca. . . .' She squeezed her eyes, waiting for the pain of a bullet to come and rip open her flesh. It didn't happen. She felt herself being lifted and then dragged across the sand. Her bare feet met with the stiff grass that dotted the small sand dunes. She was not being dragged *to* the sea but *away* from it.

The voice called to someone else. Barking out instructions, bring the body, he was saying, or something like that, she could not be certain. Her ears were still ringing with the noise of the shot.

Now there were steps, cold stone against her burning toes. He was heaving a little and must have grown tired of struggling with her down the steps, for he let her go. She bounced and rolled, but there were not that many steps and she landed in a heap at the bottom, her hip banging against a wall of some kind. Moving her feet against the stone she felt at the back of her – it was wood. He had thrown her down the tower; she had to be at the bottom of the stairs by the door that led into the passage to the palazzo. His own steps echoed down to her, but he was going back up to the top. He was not going to shoot her. . . .

Then there was a noise, something else coming down the steps, she tried to move away but it was impossible to do so. Antonio's body landed in front of her, pushing her further against the door, she was trapped with a dead man blocking any chance of escape.

CHAPTER ELEVEN

'*Cara. . . .*' The soft pink light was on, the bed covers disturbed but she was not there, the bed was empty. He went to the bathroom – it was in darkness. Still he switched on the light. He called again, as if she would pop out of a closet and it was a joke, she was hiding from him, teasing him – but Alva would not do something like that.

He went to Renata's room, quietly opening the door.

Renata was in bed, her light was still on and the television was playing, yet as he went closer to the bed he saw the girl was sleeping deeply.

Racing now along the corridor, he put on all the lights in the palazzo, calling out as he went. A sleepy Claudia came down from her room, wrapped in a huge blue bathrobe.

'Conte?'

'My wife, have you seen my wife?'

'No, Conte, not since dinner. . . .'

'Where is Carlo, find Carlo . . . quickly.'

Downstairs he ran like a demented man from room to room, servants began to appear and they, too, started to search, calling her name. Guido had thrown on a pair of jeans and little else.

'Conte?' He looked anxious. 'Carlo is not in his room.'

For a moment Luca relaxed: she had gone somewhere with

Carlo. The clock in the hall just then struck the half-hour, he looked at it ... it was one-thirty; she would have gone nowhere with Carlo.

'Get the car . . . the jeep; we have to go to the port. . . .'

Guido had the engine started up; as Luca leapt into the jeep Guido sped off down the drive.

In the car, Guido slid something towards him; it felt cold against his hand, the metal hard.

'You might need it, Conte; I took it from your gun case just in case.'

The gun felt good against his hand. He knew he would use it, if she had been harmed he knew he could kill them and think nothing about it. He could do that, he could do anything. He muttered something to Guido about what they would do but before the man could answer, Luca's mobile phone shrilled out. They had just reached the port, and leaping from the vehicle, he answered it tersely.

He listened and then, without saying anything, snapped the phone shut. 'We have to get to the shore,' he told Guido.

Guido spun the jeep around, its tyres burning up on the paving.

Alva tried to roll away; she wriggled and moved but Antonio's body, growing cold and heavy, had her pinned against the door. She was lying on her stomach; the body was almost on top of her, pressing down against her hips and legs. The bag over her head slackened if she turned her head to the side. She managed to do that, but still as she breathed in, it brushed back against her face.

Drowsiness came and went, she was afraid of it more than anything else. If she fell asleep would she smother? She must not fall asleep. Fighting sleep was difficult because whatever had been in the needle was still in her system, although it was wearing off because she was acutely aware of pain.

In her head she went through poems she knew – trying to remember all the verses was sometimes difficult, so when that happened she moved on to another one. Anything to stop the horror from mounting – she could not face what was happening. That she was trapped at the bottom of the stairs with the dead Antonio pinning her down.

'I will survive this, it's not as bad as the sea . . . I have a chance. I have to stay calm.'

She had reservoirs of mental strength, she realized. She was not a quitter so how was it that she had been so impossibly weakened when she was carrying her child? It was not like her! She was a pick-yourself-up kind of girl, dust off, start over. It would not have brought her down that much, unless, as Luca suspected, someone had been toying with her food. Making her feel ill, giving her something that would make her feel so depressed and cause her to throw up on a daily basis, even when she had supposedly passed the throwing-up weeks. But why? To keep her inside the palazzo? That is what Luca said, keep her from seeing things. Keep her out of – her body jerked with remembrance.

Something was going on, something she did not like and she suspected that Luca knew something about it.

Terrified of confronting him in case he confirmed it, not wanting to know the truth and yet wanting to know *everything*. Of course . . . that was why. . . .

There was a human sound above the rush of the tide that was now fully in. She knew that – it came close to the steps and now and again a little rush of seawater dripped in. It was a high spring tide; only on the highest tides did the water lap the edges of the fort.

It did not come right over and fill the stairwell – that much she did remember.

She recalled Luca telling her about that when he had first brought her here as his bride. He told her how, when he was a boy, he was playing and was trapped by the tide in the stairwell. The sea was not very deep but he was afraid of wading through it to get off the beach, just in case it was deep, he had crouched on the stairs in terror. It taught him a lesson and he had a respect of the sea and for the tides from that day on.

There it was again, a human sound. She shouted, when she opened her mouth to cry out it was filled with the sacking, its taste causing the bile to rise up in her throat, terrifying her with thoughts of choking on her vomit.

She lay there, listening, feeling hopeless and lost, that they would never find her because who would know to look down these stairs that were, supposedly, never used. Only she knew differently, she remembered they were used by Antonio – *frequently*.

A voice echoed down to her through the dark dampness. 'Alva . . . Alva.'

Her cry was merely a whimper – she tried to move her feet to make a noise, but it was impossible. Her feet merely hit the now-stiffened corpse of Antonio.

It was Luca up there, she heard his voice, knew the way he commanded someone. 'Bring me a torch,' he shouted. *Torcia* . . . yes, that was it, it meant torch. *Luca, hear me,* she murmured in her mind. *Look down, Luca, shine the* torcia. *Luca, see me, feel me, and know I am here.*

There was silence now, apart from the rushing tide. Dear God, he had gone, she would never get out of here. He would not come down; he would not wade through the tide, why would he ever expect to find her lying at the bottom of these steps. She would die here; hysteria mounted, she was trembling now, visions of her terrible fate coming in and out of her mind. Starvation, slow and painful, wasting away in this fetid hole with this decaying body holding her down. Dear God, it would be like being buried alive.

But no, she could not let that happen; heaving her body,

shaking herself, rocking from side to side she tried to loosen the weight of Antonio. It knocked the breath from her body but she would wait and try again. This time she bucked, lifting her legs from the floor. Somehow her legs were now free, they were between the spread out legs of Antonio. Again, she had to stop, give herself more time to rest before starting again. If she lifted her legs at the knee would it help shift the weight, would it work? What if it didn't?

It was so dark – if only she could see, if the bag were not on her head . . . but it was and there was nothing she could do.

What was that noise, a scraping sound, was it an animal? She listened, her body tense. The sound echoed again. It was a footfall. It *was* a footfall, she was sure it was. Her ears were straining to hear. She started to buck and rock again, bending her legs, hoping there was some sound.

She heard a voice echoing down to her. There were sounds that she could barely distinguish because they were couched in agony and then a wild triumphant cry. 'Guido, she's here . . . I can see her . . . get down here with me. . . .'

'Alva, Alva. . . .'

She could not move, even as the body was rolled away from her, the pain now ripped through her, the whole length of her skeleton, every bone an aching agony. She could not move.

Light, air, she gasped, then squeezed her eyes shut against the torch that was resting close to her.

'No,' she cried as he tried to lift her. 'Luca, no, a moment. . . .'

His hands were on her, soothing the pain, massaging the bruised flesh, easing her bones.

'*Cara, cara,* what have I brought you to? *Cara. . . .*'

Weakly, she indicated she would turn around and slowly her body unwound itself. She managed to stretch out her freed hands and feet. The tight bands had caused the flesh to burn; her trying to free herself had made the rope tear into the skin and there was blood oozing from the open wounds.

'Don't talk, not yet,' he murmured tenderly, now folding her to him. 'Don't speak; there,' he brushed cool finger tips over her lips. 'Stay still.'

She was aware of Guido, turning over the body of Antonio and uttering curses on the dead man.

'Leave him there,' Luca ordered. 'Let the police deal with it.'

With care and tenderness, Luca helped her up and then, sweeping her up in his arms, he started to mount the stairs. She was aware of him splashing through the rushing tide, the water just above his ankles.

The off-the-road vehicle was parked close by. She wondered if it would sink into the sand and what they would do if it did that. But as she settled on the seat in the back, Luca next to her, Guido started the engine and they moved off. He had put on the seat heater; it felt wonderful against her aching hips, the warmth soothing her spine.

'He's dead,' she said, 'the other man shot him. He was so callous, the other man, I mean. He said . . . he said "*ciao*, baby" . . . just like that. He said other things, too, that Antonio was too emotional, that he killed . . . that he murdered Rosa.'

She knew it would be an ordeal. Expected it and dreaded it and yet at the same time wanted it over with. The commisario was poised and waiting. Something about him intimidated her as if he suspected her of lying or exaggerating.

The story did not grow easier with the telling, first Luca and now this stern policeman. But it had to be done and going through it all again it seemed fanciful and far-fetched. The questions came at her like bullets. Why had Antonio wanted to kill her? What did she know that frightened him so much that he would do such a thing?

He was growing a little impatient with her; as if suspecting she was holding things back. She was and had hoped that he would not notice but he was clever in a cunning fox kind of way.

With a shrug of helplessness she looked at Luca. He took over, he explained about Renata. Alva had not wanted to say anything about that, needing to protect Renata's reputation. Oddly, the commisario was sympathetic about Renata. He had daughters; he practically shook with disgust when Luca told him what had happened. How Antonio had set about grooming the girl when she was at her most vulnerable. Of course, they knew that now. Renata, shocked by what had happened, at what Antonio had done to her stepmother had told them everything. The fact that he had pushed Alva down the stairs and caused her to lose the baby, the baby that was her half-brother, further motivated Renata to let it all out. He was dead; he no longer was able to exert any evil influence over the girl.

'So he tried to kill you before. . . .'

'I'm not sure, Commisario, whether it was just an action of anger. . . .'

'Of course he tried to kill you!' Luca said. 'It was no accident. I think you have not remembered fully what it was all about, *cara*, but you will do . . . one day. . . .'

'So . . . there is a history of *something*,' the commisario murmured, 'but now let us get to the murder of this man. You do not know who the other man was?'

She shook her head; of course, his voice had seemed familiar but she could not be certain. She told the policeman that he sounded a little like the man who had taken her on the boat, but it was not him. Of that she was sure.

'Perhaps his brother,' the commisario suggested.

'I don't know,' Alva murmured.

'But you say he accused Perseli of killing Signora d'Casta?'

'Perseli?'

'Antonio, that is his name, Antonio Perseli.'

'Oh, sorry, I didn't know. I hadn't remembered that. He did not accuse him of it, he said it. He said, you are too emotional, and something about trying to kill me and then about killing Rosa . . . I can't sort out in my head exactly what was said.'

'Did he say why?'

Her heart started to throb, she felt her cheeks burn, had she flushed up? It felt like she had.

'No,' she lied.

'You're sure?'

'I . . . I think so— remember I was lying down, the bag over my head, I might have missed something. . . .'

'You might have done,' the commisario said.

'You sound as if you don't believe any of it,' she said, not sure whether she had intended actually to say the words or just keep them in her mind.

'Of course I believe you, Contessa; I am just concerned that you are telling me everything.'

He stared at her, she returned his stare. Her mind told her, think about Luca, there is no point in knowing what they said about Renata. It would hurt him if he knew that Renata was not his daughter, it would in all probability destroy Renata were she to find out.

'I find it rather offensive that you would think that,' she answered at last, pleased to hear how cool her voice had become.

'Yes, Commisario, and so do I,' Luca had that cold authority in his voice. The commisario looked at him, a veiled look, but she could see that he had some problem with dealing with an aristocrat. That he was not impressed and intended that they knew that. So he has his own agenda, she thought, well that is nothing to us. It does not matter why the man killed Antonio, just that he did. And as to why Antonio killed Rosa, there was no need for anyone to know that.

'I want these people caught but not at the expense of making the contessa ill. I think this is enough for today. I think that it was Antonio who arranged to have her kidnapped; he must have wanted money, only it went wrong. I employed the wrong man!'

The commisario shrugged. 'It can happen. However, it is better we do it now,' he said, 'if you want these people caught.'

'We don't know who they are!' Luca said, exasperated.

'We can check who Perseli spent his time with. He has no record. How long did he work for you?'

'Seven years. I needed an assistant. He came from Firenze and he was recommended' – Luca hesitated – 'he was recommended by Rosa d'Casta.'

'Ah, you see!' The commisario said, 'you see we are getting somewhere. Everything is starting to fit into place.'

Alva was a little surprised; she had thought Antonio was long-established. That was the impression he gave and she never questioned that he had not been with the conte for longer than seven years.

When the commisario had gone she went to her room, telling Luca she going for a long soak in the bath. Her bones still ached and he understood and accepted it. She needed time to think. Desperately, she needed more time alone to go over things. Try to sort out the muddle of the past.

The water smelt heavenly of orange blossom. She lay in the bubbles, eyes closed, head resting against the cool porcelain of the tub.

Antonio, she never liked him, never took to him, something about him had her hackles rising the moment she saw him. Yet how could she tell Luca how she felt? It was a woman thing, she had nothing on him to explain her feelings.

She was, she supposed, weighing him and watching him

more than she should. She had noticed he spent a lot of time in the old building adjacent to the indoor pool.

Sometimes, when she could not sleep she would go on the balcony and gaze out. Now and again she had seen lights on the beach, a yacht in the bay. Of course it was holidaymakers. The beach was private but they probably moored and then swam out and had a party. She was not the type to go and remonstrate over something like that – it wasn't important. It was not as if it were hoards of people doing it.

Perhaps she had been seen. Often she had walked down to the beach. Luca, when she was pregnant, would not let her ride, and anyway, she had started to feel so ill she did not want to. But she knew that exercise would help her.

That was when she had gone down the stairs at the fort, curious, a little bored, and braver than she was now. The door had been partly open. She had pushed it and heard rushing footsteps.

Fearful, she had run back up the stairs, gone into the dunes and then looked back. Antonio had been there, with another man that she did not recognize. They were checking watches and looking out towards the horizon. Sure enough, around the headland a yacht had come into view. It had moored in its usual place but it was not night, it was daylight.

There was a glint of something on the yacht. Somewhere a phone had started to ring . . . she had put her hand in her pocket and then realized she had not brought her phone with her . . . and anyway the sound was too far away.

Instinct had made her throw herself down in the dip of the dune. Antonio was talking on the mobile phone. He had whirled around, looking, searching the shore. She had ducked down her head, and then slid her body down the sand. When she reached the bottom she started to run, tripping and falling through the sand as she did.

When she had arrived back at the palazzo she collided with

Luca who had been coming from the disused building. He had lost his temper, asking her what she thought she was doing running like a mad woman, her clothing and her hair covered in sand.

'Oh stop it!' she had cried, and had wrenched herself away from him. 'I don't even want to think about you!'

Whatever was going on he had to be involved. It was not innocent, she was certain of it.

From then on she had started to feel worse. Every day had brought another wretched round of sickness and lassitude. Now she saw the reason why. Even then, she had never suspected it was being done on purpose, and yet she knew that the person on the yacht had seen her. That was what the phone call had to have been about.

And she had thought Luca was involved. Did she think that now? Remember, she said to herself, try to remember if I always thought that or was it just then? Was that why I did not say anything to him, because I was always certain he was involved?

There was only one way to find out. She left the tub and dried herself, going to the closet to look for a casual tracksuit to slip into. If she confronted him – but what was she saying, confronted him? There was no need to do that because he loved her and whatever had gone on then, had to be over now. But what if . . . what if . . . I love this man and there is something sinister about him? No, she was being stupid, as usual, to think so.

Luca had been angry with her at that time. No, not angry, impatient. He had told her to do things that would make her better but she had ignored him. He had lost patience frequently. Of course she had not known that Renata was also whispering in his ear. Going to her father and telling him that his wife had a crush on Antonio. She was doing it because Antonio had ordered her to do it, just as he had ordered her not to co-operate in anyway with her stepmother. The girl confessed it all. Knowing what she did now about Silvia, she could understand how these lies must have made Luca feel. Here was another woman he could not entirely trust.

Luca came in quietly and seemed surprised she was not in bed. 'I thought you would rest. I needed to shower and change. Somehow I feel filthy after all that downstairs.'

'Me too . . . I'm not sleepy though. I relaxed in the tub.'

'Alva, is there something you are not telling me?'

The question surprised her, her mouth opened making an 'o' shape, showing that perhaps she had something to be guilty about.

'I don't think so.'

'You know you can tell me anything. . . .'

'All right. But Luca . . . it isn't entirely clear in my head. Only it's to do with when I was first here. There seemed to be a lot of coming and going, a boat would come; there would be lights at the beach. Antonio always seemed to be in the building next to the indoor pool. I watched him, I suspected him of something but I don't know what.'

He looked genuinely amazed; he raised his hands, palms upwards and asked. 'Why didn't you say? *Per Dio*, what do you think was going on? Did you imagine I was involved in something?'

'I don't know, maybe . . . I can't remember the details.'

'But what could it be, do you think he was smuggling something . . . people?'

'People? But where could he hide people? I imagine it was something much smaller.'

'Not drugs? What a vivid imagination you have, Alva.'

Alva looked at him, her head to one side. He seemed so cold, and then he went on.

'I was so busy at that time. We were developing the port, if you remember, and I was also modernizing many of the homes of my workers on the other side of the island. It was a major project; there was a lot of coming and going. I can't think he would be doing that behind my back. But of course it could be possible, I suppose.'

'It could be that. Oh Luca, I wish I had told you. I felt so ill – you seemed so distant . . . everything was going wrong and I just didn't want to. . . .'

'You did not know that I was not involved. It's all right, Alva, how could you know such a thing? That you would be married to the man who owned Santa Caterina and people were doing things behind his back. That he was too stupid to realize what was happening. That could be it . . . but I do doubt it, Alva.'

'Do you know what I think, Luca, I think you were just too trusting. You're straightforward with people and expect the same from others. I know you treat everyone very well, that people respect and love you . . . you were really the perfect person to deceive because if anyone, and I include me, even suspected you were involved in something like that, no one would have told on you.' She went to him and gave him a deep hug.

'Do you think that Rosa was involved too?' he asked quietly. 'Was her murder because of a falling out amongst thieves?'

She hesitated. But she could not do that, could not betray Renata. It was not the girl's fault that she was not his daughter. Alva, not knowing what to do, merely raised her shoulders.

He released her and went into the bathroom. He paused and asked her to order dinner. If she liked they could eat it here, out on the balcony in the peace of the warm night. Something in his attitude gave the strong impression that he did not want to talk about it, not now and not ever.

*

Later after they had eaten they sat quietly, sipping their wine and looking out over the beautiful landscape. The sea was a mass of scarlet ribbons from the burning embers of the departing sun. Drifting in on a soft breeze was the scent of a million flowers, intermingling and exotic.

'There is something else I have to tell you,' Luca said. 'I want to share this with you, and only you, you understand. It goes no further?'

'Of course. You know I can keep a secret.'

'Yes, I do know,' he smiled. 'Renata is not my natural daughter.'

She gasped, the gasp sounded so loud in the still evening air, that he looked at her curiously. '*Cara*, did I shock you that much? I'm sorry. . . .'

'How do you know?' she demanded intensely.

'I've known for years. Easy really, Renata was ill at one time and she needed blood. Mine was not deemed suitable. A child will have the same blood as its father. Later I had another check done. DNA. It was hurtful, at first, but then I realized it did not matter. You see, Renata was my daughter in practically every sense of the word. I am not a man that would reject a child because she was not from my body.'

'Oh, Luca . . . I have to come to you,' she left her seat and slipped behind his chair, embracing him deeply. 'You see each confession you make draws a confession from me. I was not honest with the commisario. Luca, I do know why Antonio killed Rosa.'

Later, when she had explained, he murmured, 'And you would keep quiet because of Renata and because of me?'

'Exactly.'

'Do you think it will make a lot of difference if we don't tell him?'

'No. What purpose would it serve as to why he killed her? He's dead, *we* know he did it,' Alva said.

'But whoever the other man is in this, he knows too? How many other people know about Silvia's secret? Silvia was a very indiscreet woman, in more ways than one,' Luca recalled.

'It's too much to share with Renata just now, anyway. If it comes out, well then we should deal with it. I think Renata has too much to contend with.'

'I agree.'

She slid on to his lap, and he held her lightly to him. 'I knew that very first day, when we spoke on the telephone. I felt you would be so special in my life and then I went and almost lost it.'

'I was horrid,' she said, 'I know that now. I can see me being so waspish, so unco-operative, yet it wasn't my fault. He must have been putting something in my food. Damn the man, he made that special time of Alessandro growing in me so unhappy and then he does that. . . .' She shivered. 'It's funny but I can't think that I even remembered exactly what happened afterwards. When I was in the hospital and everyone was fussing, for a time I thought I had tripped and fallen. Perhaps it was the fall that first started my memory's erosion and the car accident just made it worse. There's so much I still don't know. I can't even remember what I was doing in London after I left Santa Caterina. I recall I went to live outside the city. Someone had asked me to do some research, but I was really in no fit state to do it. I couldn't cope and I left. Then I went to London but why, I can't say, it won't come . . . do you think someone lured me there? Was it Antonio and his friends?'

'I don't know and you must not force yourself to think too much. Everything has been going so fast for you. You have had these devastating things happen to you . . . *Cara*, you now have to let go of it all for your own sake.'

'I will . . . but it's hard to do that – these things keep flashing in and out of my mind. Still, as long as I have you then I am afraid of nothing and no one. . . .'

CHAPTER TWELVE

THE kindest thing that Renata said was, 'I did not want to dislike you. I thought you looked nice but it was difficult. I needed to please Antonio.'

'Don't worry about it now.'

They were sitting in the car. Renata had agreed to go into the clinic voluntarily. Guido had gone to find someone to arrange for her room and to take up her bags. She had asked that Alva go with her and had said her goodbyes to her father at the palazzo.

'I didn't want to share Papa with anyone either. I had been used to it just being us.'

'None of it matters anymore, Renata, it just matters that you get better.'

'I know. You did it, Alva. Do you think I can do it too? Can I come out of this . . . this feeling . . . this misery. . . ?'

Her eyes were wide and dark and filled with a kind of fear that Alva recognized.

'It's a dark lonely place, Renata, but there is light. I promise you that you can come out the other side. Just accept their help; they do know what they are doing, even if sometimes you hate them for it.'

'You ran away. . . .'

'I know. I wish I hadn't but when your father, in an attempt to help me, said I had thrown myself down the stairs, I could not stand even to think of him.'

'I really believed him when he said he had seen you do it.'

Alva knew she was talking about Perseli; Renata never used his name any more. That had to be a positive.

'I know you did, Renata. You would not have lied about something like that. Not when it was your half-brother involved.'

'You think not?' Her mouth turned down. 'I hated the idea of having a half-brother, Alva. It was another competitor for my father's affection.'

'Here's Guido. You will be all right, Renata. Call me, talk to me, anytime.'

'You're very forgiving, Alva. I doubt I could be like that, but thank you.'

They went back to Santa Caterina using the public car ferry. Alva felt safe with Guido, safer with him really than anyone. Carlo was still her bodyguard but now that Guido was around more, she found she liked him. He had a good sense of humour and a warm heart. He talked to her and told her about his girlfriend and his hopes for his future. Carlo was quieter these days, more reflective. She felt she needed to be with someone who could make her laugh and she told her husband so.

'I am going to promote him so enjoy him while you can. I have a feeling that Guido has more to offer than just being a chauffeur-handyman. He is intelligent and he is from the island, too. He knows how things are done here.'

She did enjoy having Guido around, preferring him to accompany her on her ride and to drive her to the port, or take her across on the launch. Besides, being from the island, he had a lot of local knowledge and she determined to learn as much as possible so that she too could help her husband with the management of the island.

The day after Renata left was a perfect day, very warm and sunny. Dressing in a one-piece bathing suit, she tied a sarong to her waist and added a thin shirt for going through the house, then went down and out to the pool.

After putting her things on a sun-lounger she dived into the pool and swam several laps. Someone had been from the house while she was swimming; there was a coffee pot on the table and the umbrella had been opened over a lounger. Grateful, she slid on to the lounger, slipped her sunglasses on, and then poured coffee.

I am a little happy, she thought. *No I am* very *happy. My husband and I are in love, the darkness is in the past*. If Antonio's murderer had wanted to kill her, he would have done it when he had the chance. Even the commisario agreed on that point.

It was Antonio who had wanted her out of the way, Antonio who must have feared that she would remember everything and reveal what he was doing. Content, she fell asleep. She came to drowsily, hearing someone addressing her.

'Mm,' she murmured, her eyes still closed.

'Contessa, the conte is on the telephone. He will be late home. Apparently, one of his tenants has just died and—' *The voice!* Alarm bells rang; she felt herself shiver. Her eyes flickered open. Carlo stood at her side. Glad that the sunglasses hid her eyes, she murmured. 'Thank you, Carlo; I'll come into the house in a moment. Did you take the number?'

'I think he was on his mobile phone, Contessa.'

'Oh, of course. Thank you, Carlo.'

Cool, she thought, *be cool, stay where you are, and do not move. Your legs will tremble if you stand.* Glancing up, she saw him turn and go back towards the house.

Carlo? Carlo, whom she trusted. It could not have been him on the beach, yet the voice – concentrating on the voice and not the man, she recognized it. That slight accent. He was not a Florentine. He had lived in Florence but he was not from there, she remembered him saying. But then again so had Antonio, and Rosa d'Casta was from Florence. It all made sense – like a jigsaw, each little piece was falling into place.

The man on the boat – he, too, was from somewhere different from here. She had thought Istria or Switzerland but now when she came to think of it, his accent was not so different from Carlo's. Oh, God, had Carlo taken over from Antonio? Was there really some kind of smuggling operation and was it still going on? Of course, it would once things died down. It would start up all over again because there was so much money involved. And it was a perfect place.

Taking her time, ignoring the heavy thud of her heart, she gathered her things together and strolled back into the house. Going via the loggia she only felt safe when she slid into the sun lounge. Now in the confines of the house she knew she could rush, but she didn't. Holding herself back, first she went into the kitchen. Claudia announced that Guido was with the conte. There was no man, apart from Carlo, in the house. There were the gardeners but on this vast estate they could be anywhere.

She went to her bedroom, searching for her mobile phone. It wasn't where she usually kept it and then she remembered it had to be in her handbag. The last time she had had it with her was when she had gone to the port only yesterday. One of the designer shops had opened for the summer and she was anxious to see what kind of things they would be selling.

Her hand started to tremble. She rested it on the bed for a moment, clasping and unclasping the silken sheet. She looked at the phone by her bedside but was afraid to use it because someone would be able to hear what she said should they pick up an extension.

All her handbags were on a shelf in the walk-in closet. It

was an effort to cross the room, pull open the door and pull down the navy leather bag she had had yesterday. Snapping open the clasp she looked inside. Her phone was not there. Damn, where had she left it?

Her head started to throb; those flickering images whirled up, flashing before her eyes, things that had happened, the jumble that she could never somehow put in order. Crossing back to the bed she climbed on it and lay down. There was no reason to panic. Carlo did not know that she had recognized his voice. She was quite safe.

Carlo had not killed her on the beach. But, a little voice piped up, he had not rescued her either, he could not have cared what happened to her, just so long as he could get on with whatever he had been doing. He was a killer – he had killed once that she knew of, and he would not hesitate to kill her if he realized she had recognized him. Raising herself up, she was suddenly overcome with the feeling that she was on a merry-go-round. Her head was spinning, weakly, she sank back and closed her eyes but that made her feel nauseous. A faint tapping on the outer door had her leaping from the bed. Claudia never knocked so she knew it was not her.

It was him! He called her name. 'Contessa, are you there?'

Wildly looking around, she realized she could not hide. The bed was too close to the ground for her to dive under it, the closet was obvious. The balcony, well that was dangerous – how easy it would be for her to fall off. . . .

The passage. Tip-toeing at speed, she crossed the room, pressed the switch and as the panel gave way, nimbly stepped inside. Remembering to pull the lever to close the panel, she slid to her knees, her ear against the door.

It was dark, yet she could hear. He had opened the door and was in her room. She prayed that he did not know about the passage. The spinning of her head started to steady; closing her eyes, she felt the nausea but it was not as bad as it had been when she had lain down.

Her first thought was that there had been something in the coffee but now she was not sure. It had to be the hyperactivity of her mind that caused it.

She listened to Carlo on the other side of the panel; he was going through her room, opening drawers, going into the closet. What was he looking for? He could not know that she had recognized him. It was not that – but then, what was it?

Something was crawling on her bare leg. She jumped, running a hand along the flesh, it was small, an insect of some kind, perhaps a spider – she could not see in the dark. She brushed it off, curling up her toes with distaste.

A door closed. The door to her room, he had gone. Not trusting him, she slowly pulled herself up, then, hands braced against the walls on either side of her, she felt her way along the passageway.

A hard object knocked up against her hand, touching it, she felt its rounded rim and in the middle was a small pointed button. Breath held, she pressed it; dull light, temporarily making her eyes scorch, illuminated the passageway. She could see that she had travelled some way from her room but if she went on, with the light now on, dim as it was, she would see if there was a lever. Moving more rapidly now, it nevertheless took some time for her to locate a lever. She pulled it and a panel slid back. Stepping into the opening she saw it was her own room. She had gone round in circles. Realizing she had to have been in the dark longer than she imagined, she quickly stepped inside her room and closed the panel.

Going to the door, she opened it. The corridor was deserted; quietly she stepped out, running as silently as she could along the landing, and when she reached it, into Luca's room.

He used it very little nowadays, preferring to spend the evenings and night with her. He had shown her the safe, though. One night he had taken her to his room and shown her where her jewellery was kept so if she wanted a particular piece, she knew where it was. That is what he had said, *her* jewellery, as if it were some kind of confirmation that everything was all right now. However, she had seen something else in the safe. A small gun.

Recalling the combination more easily than her past life, she clicked open the safe. The small gun was there. She took it in her hand, as she had done that night with Luca, and he had shown her how to check for ammunition and how to remove the safety catch.

'I don't like this,' she had said, putting it back with relief.

'I don't either, but after all that has been going on I'm glad I have it.'

There was nowhere for her to hide the gun. Still wearing the flimsy sarong and top, it was impossible to put it anywhere but in her hand. But there was a place closer than her room where she could find something to wear.

She and Renata were similar in size; going to her stepdaughter's room, she went in and directly to the closet. Pulling out a pair of jeans and a shirt, she slipped out of her clothes and put these on. The gun slipped into the back pocket of the jeans and the long loose blouse hid the bulk of it.

Once downstairs she headed for the kitchen. That would be the safest place to be, there would be servants as well as Claudia, safety in numbers, but when she reached the kitchen only one person was there. It was Carlo.

'Contessa, I have been looking for you.'

'Really?'

She feigned surprise, casually tucking her hair behind her ears.

'Yes, the conte rang again; he wants me to take you to him.'

'He does? I need to call him first.'

'He said his battery is low on his phone. It will be all right, Contessa, you know that, don't you?'

'Yes, I do. It's just that we had an arrangement. I am never to go anywhere without I speak to him, you do understand?'

'But Contessa, that was when someone was out to harm you and that threat has gone.'

'I'm not sure it has. I don't want to be awkward, Carlo. . . .'

'You don't trust me? Your bodyguard?'

'It isn't that. It's just that the conte was specific, he said—'

'*Sí*, I know that, you said. But I could not find you; I came to look for you . . . where were you by the way?'

'That's none of your business, Carlo. Where is Claudia, where are the servants?'

'I imagine they are taking their rest. It is that time, is it not?' He checked his watch. 'Between two and five they are free to do as they wish.'

'Yes, but someone always stays around just in case.'

'That person is me, Contessa.'

'OK, I buy that. . . .' Casually, she slid her arm behind her back, resting her palms flat against her pockets.

'Then we shall go to the conte,' he said.

'No, I'll wait to see if he calls me. . . .'

'Contessa, I must insist. . . .'

Someone help me, she thought desperately, someone come to me now, don't let me do this, but her hand was moving quickly, sliding under the shirt, pulling the gun from her pocket, she brought her hand round and held it out. She was not certain who was the more amazed, her because her hand was steady or Carlo because of what she had done.

'Contessa, what are you doing?'

'I know who you are, Carlo. You killed Perseli.'

He relaxed, he was big and strong and somehow omnipotent and she was stupid if she imagined he would let her get away with it. But she had to try, did not want to be a victim yet again.

'Now where did that come from?'

'I recognized your voice.'

'No . . . not enough, Contessa . . . besides, I saved your life, isn't that something worth celebrating with me? That I stopped that bastard from killing you?'

'I wonder why you did that.'

'Stupid thing to do – it was bad enough that he killed Rosa, bringing cops all over the island. Imagine if he had killed you – the island would have been crawling with them. Everything is going to end – we're getting out. It's getting too hot, but he messed everything up for us. One more delivery and then I have what I want; you won't deprive me of that, Contessa.'

'What about the other man, the man on the boat?'

'Perseli's guy, nothing to do with me. But he has gone, Contessa, the way of all flesh – isn't that a saying or something?'

'You killed him too?'

'No one messes up my operation, Contessa. Not even someone as beautiful as you.'

'Sit down,' she commanded, pointing with the gun to the chair. 'We can wait for the conte to return.'

'I told you, Contessa, he is waiting for you. . . .' He laughed. 'You think it was a lie, a trick? It was no trick, Contessa; he really is waiting for you. At the port, he wants to take you somewhere special. . . .'

'That's an old story and one I am not going to fall for again.'

Carlo shrugged, 'Suit yourself, Contessa, but I assure you the conte will wait and wait . . . and then he will find a telephone and call here. No one will answer, at least not until it is too late.'

'Why not?'

'Because they are off duty till five, all of them and by five o'clock, well, we have to be gone from here by then.'

'You're going nowhere, Carlo. I do assure you of that.'

'And you think you are going to stop me, you and your little pistol. . . ?'

It was an old trick she had seen in so many films – Carlo looked over her shoulder, and his mouth turned in a faint smile.

'I told you I should take you to the conte,' he said.

'It's all right, Alva, give the gun to me.' Luca! Rather than turn her head she gave a sideways glance, it was all right, it was Luca.

'I didn't believe him . . . he's. . . .'

'I know, Alva, give the gun to me. I suddenly remembered our arrangement and knew you wouldn't forget. Now give me the gun, you don't want to hurt yourself.'

Speechless now, she handed him the gun. Luca's long-fingered beautiful hand clasped it and then let his hand drop to his side.

'But . . . but—' she began.

'I think it's time you left,' Luca said to Carlo.

'Luca, he . . . he was the man . . . on the beach, the one that shot—'

'Be quiet, Alva, you don't know what you are saying.' His voice was calm and cool, yet the effect was a like a slap across her face. Stumbling away from him, she reached out a hand for something to rest against. She came up against the huge carved dresser and leaned against it, looking up at Luca, not understanding. Not wanting to understand.

Carlo said. '*Ciao*, Luca.' He held out his hand. Luca ignored it.

'See you around sometime. . . .'

'I hope not,' Luca said.

With frightened eyes, Alva watched as Carlo swaggered out, closing the kitchen door softly behind him.

'You really should have listened to him. I wanted you away from the house.'

'I don't understand!' But she did; now she knew what it was all about. The shocking truth flashed in her mind, the memories long buried surfacing at last. Luca in the past, ignoring her warnings that something was going on. Arguing with her, being cold and unresponsive, almost brutal in his rejection of her concerns. Telling her she was being hysterical and imaginative. Of course he would have said that. He was involved. He had *known* about it all.

'You let him go,' she said, 'and he killed Antonio.'

Luca, the man she thought she loved, merely shrugged. 'Antonio was an idiot. He went too far.'

'He almost killed me.'

'Who did?'

'Carlo.'

'No he didn't. He saved you.'

'He threw me down the steps at the tower; he left me there with a bag over my head.

'He took you down the tower and dropped you from halfway down. He threw you nowhere, and you imagined it was further because of the bag over your head. You were never in real danger because I came to get you.'

'Why? Oh, Luca, why? I don't understand it; look at who you are—'

'Who I am, *cara*? I was a penniless aristocrat. My father left me this house, this island and nothing else. I have made it what it is and I had to cheat in order to get the money to do it all. I did not like what I had to do but I had to do it. Nothing is more important to me than this island and its prosperity, not even you!'

She stared at him, remembering how she had felt when she had gone out with him, how he made her feel when they made love. The magic she thought he brought into her life. It *was* a fairy tale, only the fairy tale really had an ugly side to it like, she supposed, all the old fairy tales really did.

'Look, it happened. I am sorry that Perseli got so out of control, I didn't know he would do that and then Rosa wanted to punish me because I took you back.'

'You had her killed?'

He shook his head. 'No, I didn't. That was how you heard it. Perseli was afraid that if she told you about Renata other things would come out as well. She was angry enough to tell you everything in the hope that you would leave.' He shrugged. 'As if I would have *married* the whore.'

'Did you know what he was doing to Renata?'

'Not in the past, only in the last year . . . I am not a monster.'

'You did nothing to stop it?'

He shrugged. 'She was eighteen, what could I do? Besides, she is probably going to be like her mother.'

'She's your daughter.'

'I thought we had discussed that,' he said, angry now and clipped. 'Look, Alva, it is unfortunate that you recognized Carlo, that you had to know everything – but it's over. The deal is finished. It is too dangerous and besides that I don't need the money now.'

'What are you saying, Luca?'

'That we can start again. Put all this behind us. It's all over.'

'Start again? You think I can forgive you, that I can accept that you supplied drugs, or something else?'

'I supplied nothing. The drugs were nothing to do with me.'

'You facilitated in their distribution. You let them use the island. Did you have me run over in London, Luca? Were you afraid I would tell everything I suspected.'

'No, I didn't do that. No one did that to you from here. It was an accident. Obviously you were in the wrong place at the wrong time. Just some kid probably joy-riding, who knows? It had nothing to do with us. You were gone and I knew you would not tell anyone.'

'You did?'

'What could you tell, Alva? That something was going on but you did not know what? I didn't want you to be hurt, Alva believe me – your kidnap – that was nothing to do with me.'

But she knew she could never believe him or trust him again. There was something about him, she saw now, with her eyes wide open, a cold cynicism that had always been there but she had been too blinded by love to see it. A woman in the throes of love for the first time, that was what she had been, and in that state she had brushed all her doubts to one side.

'You as good as did it,' she said, 'all of it, because you brought these horrible people into your life. That makes you just as guilty.'

'Oh, Alva, Alva, please do not be so high-minded about it. It was business. That is all.'

Pulling herself away from the dresser she looked at him with sad eyes. Aware that she could just sob, but she would not do that. She was strong now. Now she knew who she was. Moving across the kitchen she went to open the door, hesitating she turned again.

'I remember everything now, Luca. It wasn't my aunt that took my money, it was you. You said you would invest it.'

He raised an eyebrow. 'I invested it in our future, in the island. You can see the results; I am getting to where I need to be now.'

'Well then, you can send me a cheque sometime, with interest.'

'I'm sorry? I don't know what you mean?'

'You will pay me back won't you Luca? One day?'

'But of course, but you will enjoy the fruits of it all. Now we really can go places.'

She almost smiled, felt it tugging at her lips. But it would be a bitter smile, echoing the bitterness that was swelling inside her. He did not get it, thought himself so irresistible, believing that he would charm her back into his web, but twice bitten she thought . . . she had learned her lesson and learned it the hard way.

'When we first got together and Tony found out, he warned me against you. He said you were slippery and not to be trusted. He told me I should get out while the going was good.'

'I know he did. I just could not forgive him for that.'

'You set him up for his fall didn't you?'

'Of course, it was so easy, he was a stupid man.'

'Everyone is stupid who crosses you, Luca, even me. . . .'

She turned to leave.

'Where are you going?' he demanded.

'Some place,' she said, 'but I don't know yet where that place is.'

'Alva, do not be stupid, we can be together. We are wonderful together and I love you.'

She thought he meant it, just then. There was that hint of desperation in his voice, as well as that seductive quality that had lured her to him in the first place.

'Sorry, Luca, I just don't love you . . . any more.'

CHAPTER THIRTEEN

THE one thing she regretted was leaving Alessandro in his cold little grave. Yet she knew she would carry him in her heart wherever she went. She left the clothes, the jewels, everything that he had given her, apart from a pair of jeans and a blouse and jacket to travel in.

It was an extravagance to take the boat to Australia. Luca had sent a cheque, not all of her money, not even half of it, but enough to tide her over. When she received a birthday card from Australia she could not imagine who it was from. On opening it she saw it was from Chloe's parents. They wrote a letter as well, saying how much they regretted cutting her from their lives. Could she forgive them?

The letter was forwarded from the palazzo; of course Chloe's parents knew nothing of her first leaving Luca, after her fall, or her subsequent separation. She recognized on the envelope the rounded letters of Claudia. Of course, she doubted that Luca would have even bothered to forward the letter. It was fortuitous that she had written to Claudia to thank her for all she had done, and given her the address where she was living. Besides she did not even care that Luca knew where she was. She knew he would not do anything to her; he knew she would not tell anyone what had happened. She had no proof and who would believe anything against the Conte Luca San Giovanni Mazareeze.

Now she was going to go out to the people who had been like a father and mother to her. She might stay, she might not – she would think about that when she arrived in Australia.

Whatever happened, she would make a new life for herself . . . *somewhere*.

Finding a quiet corner of the deck she looked out to sea, watching the tender swell of the vivid blue Mediterranean. Inside, she felt empty and drained of emotion. The love she had felt for Luca had shrivelled and died. She could not love a man that she did not respect. He had made it easy for her to get over him, but sometimes, in the dark of night she remembered moments of tenderness shared . . . they would stay with her for some long time but did not fill her with longing to be with him again.

Whatever the future held she knew it had to be better than the past. She was at heart an optimist; things could not be bad forever, nothing, after all, lasted forever, even love . . . she smiled, now that was cynical and she was not going to let Luca or anyone else turn her into a cynic.

The soft warm breeze brushed against her cheeks, bringing with it the promise of *something* . . . but she did not know what.